A.M. Burrage - Warning Whispers & Other Stories

Alfred McLelland Burrage was born in Hillingdon, Middlesex on 1st July, 1889. His father and uncle were both writers, primarily of boy's fiction, and by age 16 AM Burrage had joined them. The young man had ambitions to write for the adult market too. The money was better and so was his writing.

From 1890 to 1914, prior to the mainstream appeal of cinema and radio the printed word, mainly in magazines, was the foremost mass entertainment. AM Burrage quickly became a master of the market publishing his stories regularly across a number of publications.

By the start of the Great War Burrage was well established but in 1916 he was conscripted to fight on the Western Front. He continued to write during these years documenting his experiences in the classic book War is War by Ex-Private X.

For the remainder of his life Burrage was rarely printed in book form but continued to write and be published on a prodigious scale in magazines and newspapers. In this volume we concentrate on his supernatural stories which are, by common consent, some of the best ever written. Succinct yet full of character each reveals a twist and a flavour that is unsettling.....sometimes menacing....always disturbing.

There are many other volumes available in this series together with a number of audiobooks. All are available from iTunes, Amazon and other fine digital stores.

Table Of Contents

Warning Whispers

Beach and Dolby were hanged at the County Gaol at eight o'clock on a Thursday morning; and the village, if it made somewhat more than a nine days' wonder of the crime, slowly reassumed its normal air of sleepiness. Indeed, as Beach and Dolby were not natives, but casual labourers who had strayed thither from the teeming port some thirty miles distant, only one or two of the villagers were closely concerned with the tragedy. One of them was Martha Speed, the mother of the poor murdered girl.

John Archelaus Hoskins was probably the person most closely and lastingly affected. For one thing, he was the hero of the hour; and for another, he was one of the very few to whom good had been blown by this particular ill-wind. It was his evidence which had tied the nooses around the necks of Messrs Beach and Dolby, and it was he, or rather his mother, who received the reward of one hundred pounds, which had been, perhaps, a little too hastily offered. At the time he was a very promising boy of eight.

Nothing could shake young Hoskins's testimony. Certainly the two barristers could neither bully him nor cast a doubt upon his word. He was clear, cool, intelligent, and his little piping voice penetrated to the farthest corner of the hushed court. As he was passing Tumbledown Bam he had heard two men coming out, and had hidden behind the opposite hedge until they were gone. He had hidden because he had been poaching trout in Squire Pollard's stream, and he didn't know who was coming. He recognised Beach by the black patch he wore over his left eye, and Dolby by his stoop and slight lameness.

He had seen the two men dabble their hands in a ditch not twenty yards from where he was hiding, and heard one say—he didn't know which—'You'll 'ave to burn that coat o' yourn.'

Small wonder, in the circumstances, that John Archelaus Hoskins, the orphaned son of a butcher's assistant, became the hero of his native village. An older head than his might easily have been turned, for there was not a man, woman, or child but made much of him. In a community of thick-wits his precocious intelligence shone like a candle flame in a dark room.

Three days after the trial old Squire Pollard came plodding down the village street on a cob which looked ridiculously small for him. He was elderly—a childless widower, and something of an eccentric. It pleased him to appear in public looking like a small farmer on the verge of bankruptcy, but he was well known to have more money than he could conveniently spend. Narrow and fanatical in his religious views, he was also hard and mean in nine-tenths of his dealings, but indulged now and then in surprising bursts of generosity.

Outside Mrs Hoskins's cottage he dismounted, and was received by the smirking matron, who dusted a chair for him in the front room and fussed around him like a distracted hen.

'Well, Mrs Hoskins,' said he, 'all the excitement over now, eh? Settling down again to ordinary everyday life? Excitement bad for all of us. How's the boy?'

'Oh. 'e's at school, sir,' said Mrs Hoskins. "E's still a bit excited-like. But we can't expect old 'eads on young shoulders, can we, sir?'

The squire nodded. 'He's a smart lad for his age,' he said, thoughtfully.

'Ay, 'e is that, sir. 'E's the apple of 'is mother's eye. You wouldn't believe what a good boy 'e is.'

'Hum! I have an idea he'd been poaching in my stream when he saw those two miscreants'

'Ah, sir, if I'd only known that at the time! But we can't expect old 'eads on young shoulders, as I said before, can we, sir? And if 'e 'adnt' been fishin' that evenin''

Squire Pollard nodded again.

'Just so! Poaching's wrong, though. Wicked. Stealing. Still, we'll say no more about that.'

'Thank you, sir. The pore little man's been punished enought already. 'E can't get out of 'is 'ead the way them two villains scowled at 'im while 'e was givin' evidence against 'em. 'E 'ad a nightmare about it last night. I'm sure, sir, if they could do 'im a mischief they would.'

The squire smiled wryly.

'Well, they'll never be able to hurt young John or anybody else. Make him understand that. When do you expect him back from school, Mrs Hoskins?'

'In about 'alf an hour, sir.'

'Very well, I'll wait. Does he know his catechism?'

The woman smiled broadly.

'Why, sir,' she said, 'you examined the children yourself and give my Jacky first prize.'

'Bless me! So I did. Knows his catechism, eh? Well, I've been thinking! He seems a very bright boy indeed. Ought to have a real chance in life. I don't want to take him away from you, Mrs Hoskins—only to go away to school. And I'll see you don't lose by it. I haven't a son of my own' He broke off abruptly and hitched his cloth gaiters. Mrs Hoskins flinched and coloured as if the hand of prosperity had struck a sudden blow at her.

' 'E's a good boy,' was all she could say.

When Master Hoskins arrived home half an hour later, kicking another boy's cap down the garden path, he was surprised to find an august presence in the front room.

'Come here,' the squire greeted him. 'Come here and tell me what happened in 1815.'

'Battle o' Waterloo, sir,' said Master Hoskins, promptly.

The year before a very much older boy had received a shilling from Squire Pollard for answering the self-same question. Since then not a boy in the village but knew the date, for other shillings might be forthcoming. But the squire had forgotten, and the triumph of John Archelaus Hoskins was complete.

Next day, when the new favourite of fortune met Anne Peters, a damsel of his own years, he haughtily declined to play with her.

'I shan't be able to play with you no more, Anne,' he said. 'Haven't 'ee heard as Squire Pollard be goin' to make a gentleman of me?'

Miss Peters put out her tongue at him and made a remark which would have staggered her Sunday School mistress.

'Mother says,' she added, 'that your luck come to you by an evil road and you'll get no good of it.'

'Sour grapes!' retorted young Hoskins.

The first step towards raising young Hoskins from the level of the peasantry was taken at once. He was provided with stiff clothes and made to wear every day the hard, wide collars he had hitherto worn only on Sundays. He was then sent to a distant vicarage, where a large family of children bullied him and derided him until his nouns agreed with his verbs and, bit by bit, he lost most of his broad country accent.

At the age of ten he was sent to an establishment where boys were prepared for the Navy and the Public Schools. There he gave out that his parents were both dead and that he was the nephew of Squire Pollard, a most important man, from whom one day he would inherit several millions of pounds. That kind of braggadocio was, however, kicked out of him before he was ready to take another step.

Squire Pollard had entered the boy at Charterhouse, but, when he was fourteen, and ready to sit for the entrance examination, the old man had a sudden fit of economy, and young Hoskins was despatched to King Edward the Sixth School, Somewhere-or-Other.

It was a good school, although inexpensive, and its endowment provided for half a dozen scholarships at Oxford and Cambridge. Young Hoskins, at the age of eighteen, took one to the value of one hundred pounds per annum, and duly went up to one of the smaller colleges at Cambridge.

The scholarship was his crowning triumph in the sight of the squire, who was now turned seventy and beginning to feel his years. He regarded the young man more than ever as a son, and sent him up to the University with an allowance which he regarded as princely, and which really was quite reasonable.

Meanwhile young Hoskins had spent half his school holidays with his mother and half at the Hall. Old Mrs Hoskins, who had a gift for attracting charitable notice, now occupied a very superior cottage, and imitated the dress and manners of the vicar's wife. Squire Pollard had duly seen that she lost nothing by the partial surrender of her son. She was painstaking, if not always correct, in the use of her aspirates, and inclined to patronise her less fortunate neighbours.

The village had not forgotten the murder, but it had grown used to the distinction conferred by it. Tumbleweed Barn was still pointed out to strangers, and, of course, it achieved a reputation for being haunted. One night, in the long vacation at the end of his first year at Cambridge, young Hoskins was standing at the door of the superior cottage, talking to his mother. He was then just twenty, and had grown into a tall, slim youngster with nothing of the stolid heaviness of his labouring forebears apparent in his build. Dark-haired, dark-eyed, and rather pale, he had his full share of good looks, and these were of a softer and more feminine type than one would have expected after seeing the photographs of the bright boy about whom all England had talked for a day.

'Who is she, mother?' he asked, with a careless nod towards the back of a girl who had just passed the gate.

'She? You used to know her once. You used to play with her when you was both children. But you've forgotten her now. And very right you should. I'm sure.'

'That's not her name, mother,' he said, laughing.

'To be sure. Her name's Anne Peters, and a nice, fast piece of goods she is too, I've heard.'

'Anne Peters!' He was stroking his chin as old men stroke their beards, I remember, of course. I'm afraid we quarrelled after—that. She's grown up rather pretty.'

Mrs Hoskins sniffed.

'I hope,' she said, 'my Jacky won't have any truck with the likes of her. The squire wouldn't like you to mix with village people.'

He laughed, and bent to kiss her.

'You needn't worry, mother,' he said, I wouldn't offend the old boy for worlds. Besides, I prefer the society of ladies.'

'You're not going out now?'

'Yes. I promised I'd look the old boy up before he went to bed, and he goes pretty early now. I shan't be long.'

He disappeared into the dusk, and his way happened to be up the hill whither Anne Peters had gone.

'Anne!' he called to her, softly. 'Anne!'

She turned and saw him abreast of her, his hat lifted.

'Don't you remember me, Anne?' he asked, with a little laugh.

'It's Mr Hoskins,' she said.

'I thought you'd forgotten.'

'I thought you'd forgotten, Mr Hoskins. What do you want with me?'

She did not speak at a cultured pitch, but her accent was almost pure. Like many village girls of this generation, she had striven after that mysterious thing which she called refinement.

'Nothing,' he said, in answer to her question. 'But we're going the same way, and we're old friends. Won't you let me walk with you?'

He saw her profile cut clear in the faint light which pierced the ragged foliage overhead. Almost Greek it was, to an eye already critical of women, save that the chin was a thought too prominent and the lips were pouting.

'I can't stop you, can I?' she asked. 'But you're a gentleman now. Why do you want to walk with me?'

'Where are you going?' he asked, ignoring her question.

'Never you mind.

'Is it to meet somebody?'

'Perhaps. Why?'

'Only because I'm jealous, Anne.'

She laughed quite prettily. She could take a hand in this game as well as he.

'You're at Cambridge college, aren't you?' she asked. 'Do they learn you to flirt there?'

'It's a natural gift. I've been taught, however, to recognise beauty when I see it. You're a lovely kid, Anne. I expect a dozen of these louts have told you that a hundred times.'

'It doesn't follow as I believe them.'

'But you believe me. I'm an expert.' He laughed, and linked his arm in hers. 'You're not going out with any of these ticks tonight. You're coming for a walk with me.'

Her quick little brain busied itself in an instant with a hundred possibilities. Nowadays the village despised young Hoskins for a gentleman who was not a real gentleman. But there was glamour about him—a nice surface polish—and one day he was going to be very rich. If a girl were only clever enough

'What would squire say,' she inquired, archly, 'if he knew you were taking me out?'

'What the eye doesn't see—you know, Anne.'

She made a half-hearted attempt to rid herself of his arm. 'There you are!' she said. 'He wouldn't like you to be flirting with a girl like me.'

'I don't see eye to eye with him in everything. He ought at least to admit my good taste, Anne. You are a dear, you know.'

He disengaged his arm from hers, and this time slipped it around her waist. She, on her part, let her head fall back against his shoulder, as she would have done with any other rustic swain with whom she walked on a dark evening. Thus they descended the hill to where a five-barred gate gave entrance to a farmyard, and, close to one of the granite posts a black barn thrust one of its comers through the ragged hedge.

Anne halted, and brought him to a halt.

'You remember?' she asked.

'God! Yes!' He drew and expelled an audible breath. 'There's the spot over there where I hid that night.'

'Have you been inside?' she whispered.

'Never since. Come on.'

She uttered a little provoking laugh.

'You're as nervous as a thoroughbred!' she exclaimed, and he affected to ignore the double meaning. 'They say the place is haunted. You don't believe that, do you?'

'It ought to be!'

'What? You at Cambridge College and believe in ghosts?'

'Why not? There are a lot of men up at Cambridge who do. There's a little society of us who investigate such things, and I can tell you there is a lot in it. There's a Scotsman up at Trinity who is what they call a clairvoyant. Do you know what he told me, Anne?'

She shook her head. She was smiling, and her eyes were full of amusement and unbelief—tenderly contemptuous they looked in the dusk. 'He told me, Anne,' young Hoskins continued, in a strained, hushed voice, 'that two evil spirits dogged me, seeking to hurt me. One took the shape of a man with a black patch over his eye. Do you remember Beach, or were you too young?'

She nodded, but she was still smiling.

'The Scotchman knew about you,' she said, 'and tried to frighten you.'

'No. Nobody up there knows that I'm the boy who got those two fellows hanged.'

Anne plucked at his sleeve.

'Come and peep inside.'

'No. The dog would bark and rouse people.'

'They keep him the other side, where the fowls are.'

'Aren't there fowls roosting in the barn?'

'They say fowls won't roost there. There's only a couple of old carts and some straw.'

'Anne,' he whispered, 'the place *is* haunted!'

'Are you afraid to peep inside—even with me with you?'

'Of course not! Only I -'

'Come on, then!'

Unwillingly he pushed open the farm gate and led the way on tiptoe to the door of the Tumbledown Barn. He held the door open for her to enter first, and followed, striking a match.

The barn smelt damp within, and was in an advanced stage of disrepair. The faintly luminous sky shone through a dozen gaps in the roof. The match, flaming bravely in the still air, lit up the place and showed the two old farm carts, a litter of old rubbish, a pile of straw.

Hoskins lit another match when the first burned out. His hand was not quite steady.

'Why don't they burn the place?' he demanded, in a harsh whisper, it's full of evil! I can feel it! Can't you feel it too? Oh, let's go!'

'Why,' said Anne, 'you're afraid.'

'Only because I understand—and feel! They're here—Beach and Dolby!

Don't you feel that the place is devil-ridden? It's bad—bad! I could be cruel here—cruel as hell—damnably cruel! I could'

He broke off suddenly. Before the match went out the girl could see little spots of moisture shining on his brow.

'Why,' she whispered, with a little, soft, wheedling laugh, 'you don't want to hurt me, do you?'

She stood before him, dimly revealed in the deep gloom. The soft bright in her eyes mocked the light of love. The shadows which hid part of her beauty hinted at an even richer loveliness. Something in him, beyond his control, responded to the silent call of her.

'Hurt you?' he heard himself cry. I hurt you? I who love you—love you—love you! Little Anne!'

His arms were around her. His lips found hers and clung to them. In the darkness she gave him kiss for kiss, until she felt his body start like a hooked fish, and he seized her and blundered wildly with her towards the gleaming rectangle of the open door.

'Didn't you hear?' he stammered as he faced her, gasping, in the clean air outside. 'Oh, God, didn't you hear? Somebody laughed!'

When Hoskins finally came down from Cambridge two years later, he went to stay with Squire Pollard, whose remaining days were not many. The old man had already spoken to Hoskins quite openly about his will.

'I hope you'll take the old name when I'm gone,' he said. 'You're fit to bear it. You're a clever boy, and I think you've been a good boy. Only one breath of scandal about you has reached my ears, and that I wouldn't believe.'

There was a hard light in old Pollard's eyes, and the younger man coloured uncomfortably. 'What was that, sir?' he asked.

'Oh, never mind! People wag their tongues a deal too much. I've already told you I don't believe 'em. If I did, you wouldn't set foot across this threshold again. I'd not go to my God—as soon I must—and have to admit that I'd connived at wickedness in others. A hussy like that Anne Peters deserves to be '

'Ah!'

'What do you mean by "Ah!"?'

Young Hoskins knew how to assume the role of an injured innocent.

'Because I've spoken to her when I've met her out!' he exclaimed, 'I suppose that was enough to start a rumour in this scandal-whispering hole. I used to play with her when we were both children. Thanks to you, sir, my position's changed since then. But one doesn't like to cut people one used to know. It would seem too foolish and snobbish, since not a soul in the village but knows my history.'

The old man nodded, and the younger one wished his eyes were not so alert and keen, i shouldn't speak to her anymore,' he said. 'It is her own fault if she has placed herself beyond the pale.'

The conversation ended there, but a new dread was born in the young man's heart. Except for an accident, old Pollard's money was now as good as his own. He told himself that he had been a fool to risk so much for this rustic light-o'-love who, after all, had served no more than to dispel some of the dullness of his vacations.

For a long time past he had contemplated breaking off his association with Anne Peters. Now he saw the necessity for such a step. If rumour grew into a circumstantial story, built up out of evidence, he knew' old Pollard's will would be in the fire and a new one drafted. For a man who firmly believed that he was dogged by two evil spirits which were determined to compass his ruin, he had to admit to himself that he had behaved like a fool. So, on the following night, when he went to meet Anne Peters at Tumbledown Barn, he had decided that it was for the last time.

Of course, he expected trouble. Anne would object to being cast off, and he might have to make her a present in money. This, although he was not famous for being open-handed, troubled him very little, since he had over three hundred pounds in the bank, which he had thriftily put by out of his allowance. All he needed to do was to keep her quiet temporarily until the breath was out of his benefactor's body. He might even make her a vague promise of subsequent marriage which he need not fulfil.

It was as if by some queer process of telepathy Anne Peters was aware of his intention that night, and had determined to profit herself by striking the first blow. He saw that something was amiss with her while he stood in the entrance to the barn, a lighted match between his hollowed hands. She did not trip towards him and offer to kiss him, as was her wont, but sat aloof on the dropped pole of an old wagon.

'You're late, as usual,' she greeted him. 'You're late every time. It's no way to treat a lady. I suppose you're afraid to be here a minute by yourself. Afraid the ghost with a patch over his eye will get you!'

He grimaced at this loose reference to one of his personal devils in that of all places. Then he smiled, and, as he struck another match, managed to answer lightly, 'What's the matter with you, old thing? You've got a grouch on you tonight.'

'I'm sick of it all,' she answered. 'Sick and tired.'

So was he, but he could not say so. His voice mocked the accents of a lover as he crossed the barn towards her.

'Poor little old Anne! Never mind, poor little girl. Very soon now'

She stood up and faced him purposely. He could see that she had been lashing herself into a fury by the mental repetition of her real or assumed grievances.

'For God's sake, don't give me any more promises!' she cried, I've been listening to 'em, off and on, for two years, till I'm sick. Promises aren't solid things to live on—yours especially! I've had enough of it.'

'Anne!' he exclaimed.

'Yes, Anne!' she mocked.

'What do you want?'

'What I'm going to get. You're going to marry me.'

'Of course,' he murmured. 'Some day.'

'Not someday. At once.'

Fear began to tingle in his blood. He leaned against one of the wheels of the wagon and avoided meeting her eyes in the gloom.

'Is there any reason,' he asked, 'why we should be married soon?'

A moment elapsed before she answered: 'Yes.'

'That's a lie,' he said; and he knew suddenly in his heart that she was lying. A sudden fury shook him, for that she should try to deceive him—a man of the world, as he accounted himself—by this threadbare trick.

'Lie or not,' she answered, 'you'll marry me within three days, or you'll regret it.'

It was strange how suddenly he hated her, how hard he found it to school his tongue in replying.

'Then you'll marry a pauper. He'll disinherit me.'

'Because I'm not good enough for you?' she sneered. 'Because I'm a common girl and you're a gentleman?'

She had stung him again. In cold fury he answered: 'Don't hold me responsible for his views. Why can't you wait until he's dead? It won't be long.'

She broke out into ironic laughter. 'You think I'm a fine fool, don't you? I don't want your promises. You'll marry me in three days, Jack Hoskins.'

'He'

'He needn't know. We can be married by licence over at Towcester.'

'That couldn't be done in three days.'

'Haven't you heard of a special licence?'

He turned at bay then, openly savage.

'Why can't you wait until he's dead?'

'Because a dead man can't alter his will. A lot you'd care then! Do you think I don't know you? You'll marry me within three days or I'll go to him and tell him everything.'

Vaguely he was aware that his control had slipped from him. He was like a ridden horse mastered by strange hands. Feebly he strove against something that he knew to be evil. When he answered it was as if he listened to a strange voice which spoke for him.

'Of course, he'd take your word against mine!'

'He'd have to, with the letters I've got to show—the letters posted from Trumpington, in case anybody in the village should see the Cambridge postmark.'

'Anne! Anne!' He heard the name slide out of his mouth all oily and wheedling. 'You wouldn't ruin me, would you, Anne?'

She mocked him, mincing her accent in imitation of his. Strange, he thought, that she did not realise her peril; strange that she did not see the change in him. He felt himself moving in a black cloud which should have been visible to her. It seemed to him that the darkness around him was riven continually by small, swift flashes of light, so that he saw eyes watching him, grinning lips, twisted, malevolent features which he remembered across the years. For one immeasurable fraction of time he was back in the witness-box; his little, piping voice filled the great room; and these same eyes which gloated over him now shot hatred at him across the well of the court. Anne was speaking again. He could hardly hear her. There were voices whispering to him that if she were dead she couldn't speak at all—couldn't even tell old Pollard the story of this liaison. Her words blent with these whisperings into a murmurous babble.

'You never meant to marry me!' he heard her say.

'Marry you!' Was it his own voice—that sneering snarl? 'You, a village slut with a kiss for every Tom, Dick, and Harry! Marry you!'

She would have answered him in kind, but he had drawn near to her; and in the gloom she saw his face, all wrung and devilish.

'Jack!' she cried. And in that, the last coherent word she ever uttered, there was a wail of terror and dismay.

Presently it was all so still and silent that the rats came out of their refuge in the heap of straw.

Next morning the village was electrified.

All previous excitement was surpassed a thousandfold when it became known that Tumbledown Barn had claimed a second victim; that Anne Peters had been strangled there, and that 'Mr Hoskins' had been arrested in connection with the crime.

A hundred rumours were current during the day. Among them, the most persistent and—as subsequent events proved—the best founded, was to the effect that Hoskins had already confessed. At six o'clock the tap-room of the inn was filled by an eager crowd of yokels, most of whom remembered the previous crime, all eagerly discussing the new sensation.

Old Gaudy, the badger, voiced the sentiments of most of the others.

'I mind them other two very well,' he said. 'Beach with his one eye, and Dolby with his stoop and shamblin' limp. Bad men they was both, as most of us knowed from the moment they set foot in the village. But who'd ha' thought it o' young Hoskins? Why, not a man or woman here that thought him worse nor a stuck-up calf! Truly the ways of men be past understanding.'

The entry of the village policeman created a hubbub in the crowded bar. Police Constable Clark had been absent all day at the county town, whither he had taken his prisoner. He was new to the neighbourhood, and therefore able to be more impressive than a native. With promotion already within his grasp, he entered the house with a swagger which was almost pardonable. He was the man of the hour.

'I can't tell none o' you nothing,' he said, as he accepted a pint of beer, and made his voice carry above the clamour of a score of questioners. 'It ain't accordin' to regulations. You'll hear all about it in good time.' For five minutes he was adamant, until Seeley, the grocer, spoke to him.

'But Mr Clarke,' he said, 'if it be true that you went into the barn and found him in the act of burying the body in the straw—that's what we've heard tell—what made you go to the barn at all?'

The constable coughed and expanded his chest.

'I don't mind tellin' you that,' he said, 'as there's two missin' witnesses I've got to make inquiries for, and p'raps some o' you can put me on the right road. Not as these 'ere witnesses are necessary in view of what's happened, but it's regulations. Two men came round to my cottage yesterday evenin' and told me there was trouble up at the barn. Two tramps, I think they was. Leastways, I haven't seen them hereabouts. They'd gone by the time I'd got my boots laced, and I didn't see 'em very clearly through the window.'

'Wot was they like, these two?' questioned Seeley.

The constable considered.

'Well,' he said at last, 'it seemed to me that one wore a black patch over his left eye, and the other 'ad stoopin shoulders and seemed to limp.'

The Attic

Before the war, Stanley Forbes and Raymond Telford used to play Rugby football together for a small and unimportant club, now defunct, which rented a playing-pitch near Wimbledon. They had nothing very much in common, save that they formed the left wing of the three-quarter line, and shared common triumphs and failures every Saturday afternoon during the season.

The club consisted mainly of young men who had 'jobs' in London offices and had more money to spend at the weekends than at any other time. After matches it was customary for the team to pay a protracted call at the nearest house of entertainment, and afterwards go up to the West End, there to dine inexpensively and go on to a music-hall. They saw little of one another save on the field, and at these subsequent mild debauches.

However, Forbes and Telford discovered that only the length of a short street separated their respective business premises, and this led to their lunching together two or three times a week, talking of past and forthcoming matches, and working out schemes for attack and defence. Forbes worked in the office of a firm of chartered accountants, and Telford was articled clerk to a long established firm of solicitors. They were of much the same age, their prospects in life were about equal, and, in a quiet, unostentatious way, each was more than a little impressed with his own importance. It is more than likely that the tacit rivalry between them was at the root of this casual friendship. They never boasted openly to each other of what they had done or were going to do; there was a slight strain of subtlety in both of them; but each was firmly convinced that he was the better man and would wrest more out of the world than the other.

It is more than likely that the memory of this old rivalry, after a decade had passed, was the cause of Telford suddenly writing to Forbes and inviting him to come down and stay with him for a week or two. Telford had come into money, and had bought a partnership in a firm practising at Horlington, in the New Forest. He was proud of the big house he had recently bought and the pretty young wife he had recently married.

The war, which had killed the football club—and, incidentally, most of its members—had separated Forbes and Telford. They were gazetted to different regiments, and came out with honours easy, each having won the MC and attained the temporary rank of captain. Neither played football again after the war. They were getting 'thirty-ish', when most men prefer to become spectators; and Telford had in his leg that which put an end to all serious athletics. Having settled in the Moat House, which stood actually in the Forest, whence he drove himself to the High Street office every morning and afternoon, he fell to wondering how 'old Forbes' was getting on, and at last, obeyed an impulse to write and ask him and invite him down. That was in the spring of 1924.

Forbes was not at all averse to meeting Telford and comparing notes. He was unmarried, but unlikely to remain so indefinitely, and he, too, could boast of some success. He also was now a partner, and his firm, which specialised in making war on the income-tax commissioners, was prospering exceedingly. He was overdue to take a holiday, and he accepted the invitation very much in the spirit in which it was made. He drove himself down in a brand-new car on the Tuesday of the week preceding Easter.

If there had once been a moat around Telford's house, there was no sign of it now. Instead, there was an old red wall, ten feet high or more, up which closely trimmed ivy climbed in places, which completely hid house and gardens from the road and lent the place not so much an air of privacy as one of secrecy. The wide gates were of solid timber set in an arch; and a little door further down the wall—which, when open, showed nothing more satisfying than a path which lost itself immediately in a dense shrubbery—gave access to servants and tradesmen.

'Pretentious, but dark and damp, I should think,' thought Forbes, as he got out of the car and pushed open the heavy gates.

On the inside was a small lodge, and a woman came out to close the gates behind him as he drove through. The house, just visible through the fledgling trees, was scarcely fifty yards distant. He followed the windings of the short drive, and came to a halt on fresh gravel before the front door. The house was long, three-storied, creeper-clad, and of a slightly depressing aspect. Forbes recognised Jacobean architecture, and at the same time wondered what a lawyer in a country practice could want with a house of such a size. For one idle moment he speculated on its past and on the intentions of those who had designed and built it. While nobody but an estate agent could have described it as a country mansion, it was too large to be called a hunting-box. Then the door opened and Raymond Telford, looking scarcely a day older after ten years, came out with a grin of welcome and a cheery hail.

An hour later, over tea in the drawing-room—dispensed by the frail, dainty wisp of a girl who had been Mrs Telford for the past two years—he learned how his host had come to acquire the house.

'Of course,' said Gladys Telford, 'we and the furniture are simply lost here. We don't use the top floor at all, and keep it empty except for one attic which we use as a box-room. The servants sleep on the same floor as ourselves, in order to save work. It's a lot too big for us, but we shan't be here for ever. We shall be selling it.'

'I'm hoping to make a clear couple of thousand on the deal before I've done,' remarked Telford, with quite his old air of suppressed but conscious cleverness.

'I hope you'll prosper to such an extent that you'll soon find it too small for you,' Forbes said.

Gladys laughed.

'I'm afraid not. We're a very modest couple. At least, I'm trying to teach Ray to be modest. But, of course, when he decided to go into business in Horlington we had to find somewhere to live, and it wasn't so easy as it seems. As a residential district this part of the world is enjoying something of a boom. We found that there were practically no moderate-sized houses to be had, and those on the market were an appalling price. And this place was as cheap for its size as the smaller houses were dear.'

'Most people,' explained Telford, 'are poor nowadays, and they've got to think about upkeep and servants. They find it saves 'em money in the long run to pay a bit extra for a small place and save on the cost of running it. Houses of this size, which are too big for the New Poor and not big enough for the New Rich, are a bit of a drug on the market.'

'And Ray thought,' continued Gladys, obviously proud of her husband's acumen, 'that if we bought this place cheap and lived in it for a while, values would begin to readjust themselves. We could then sell the Moat House at a profit and buy a small house for very much less than we should have to pay now. Without using the top floor, it's not a difficult house to run. I manage quite well with two maids.'

Telford gave Forbes that quiet, knowing smile which, in the old days, had always reminded him of a wink, and Forbes laughed and said:

'You were always steeped in low cunning. But when the time comes you won't be able to persuade Mrs Telford to go. It's too charming.'

He had already been over the house, and he spoke sincerely. It was melancholy, but still charming. It was rich in beams and panels, and these things Forbes reverenced. For a permanent residence he preferred a modern house, but it was only right and proper that he should have friends who were able to provide him with a complete change.

'You don't feel that it's like a prison, then?' Mrs Telford asked.

'Like a - Oh, you mean the wall? Well, on the outside I did rather wonder. But one doesn't seem to notice the wall here. Does it go completely all round?'

'Oh, yes. At the back there's just a little wicket gate which leads into the orchard and pitiable-looking broken bottles cemented to the top. I wonder who built it, and why?'

'Some old guy who got fed up with the sight of his fellow men, I suppose,' Telford laughed. 'I wonder how young Derek will like it. That reminds me. Tomorrow, my dear!'

Mrs Telford smiled.

'I hadn't forgotten. The three-eighteen train, isn't it? You've a fellow guest, Mr Forbes, and I hope you won't let him bore you. My young brother is coming home from school. Fie hasn't had a home of his own since mother died, so he goes around spending his holidays with different relatives. This is his first visit here.'

'Good,' said Forbes. 'I like boys. How old is he?'

'Fifteen,' Telford said. 'He's at Hurlborough, and he's going to cost me a fiver if he gets Seconds at cricket this year, which I think he very likely may.

He's a bright lad. If you know anything about wireless or electricity, for heaven's sake don't let on to him, or he'll plague the life out of you.'

'I'll retaliate,' said Forbes, 'by telling him all about accountancy.'

After tea, Telford took out his two-seater and bore the guest away to the little Country Club in Horlington, where the elite, consisting mostly of retired warriors, assembled to play bridge in the early evenings.

On the way home for dinner, Forbes said, 'It's suddenly struck me. If you ever do sell that house I know exactly who you'll sell it to.'

'Who?'

'Somebody who's going to start a school.'

Telford laughed over the steering-wheel.

'That's rather bright of you,' he said. 'I'd thought of that already. Matter of fact, it has been a school. Years and years ago, though, and not within living memory. Not much chance of the kids breaking out, eh?'

Dinner was a little more elaborate than Forbes had expected. He knew instinctively that his hosts lived more simply when they were alone, and the succession of courses secretly annoyed him, not merely because they hinted at vulgar display, but because he realised that they must have cost his hostess a great deal of trouble. Gladys Telford was very jolly and simple, and he wanted her somehow to be made aware that all this fuss on his behalf was quite unnecessary. But Telford was a good host, and after Gladys had crossed the hall to the drawing-room he crowned the evening by producing an old vintage port and a very old brandy.

It was when they were on their way to rejoin Gladys that Forbes halted in the middle of the hall and stood listening.

High up, and coming seemingly from the very roof of the house, he heard the shaken, rending sound of a child sobbing. The sounds varied. Sobs became a low wail, ending in a paroxysm like a muffled scream, changing again to hard, tearing sobs. Infinitely distressing, with their suggestion of the direst bodily or mental anguish, the sounds came straight to him down the well of the staircase.

'Good Lord!' he exclaimed. 'What's that?'

'That,' said Telford with a chuckle, 'is our ghost.'

He pinched Forbes's elbow and gave him a gentle push towards the drawing-room.

'Stanley's just been hearing our ghost,' he remarked to Gladys, who had risen to ring for the coffee.

'Yes,' she said indifferently, 'I noticed it as I came through.'

Forbes looked from one to the other and laughed weakly.

'But what on earth is it?' he asked, it sounds exactly like a child'

'I know! I know! It frightened us to death when we first heard it.'

'It's a ghost,' said Gladys, turning away from the bell, 'that comes to warn us. But that's quite usual among ghosts, isn't it?'

Forbes smiled, and continued to look puzzled. They were plainly teasing him.

'But what is it?' he asked. 'And what does it warn you against?'

'Rain,' said Telford, it means that the wind's gone round to the south or west. Our ghost is actually a chimney-cowl which needs something done to it. When it spins one way it doesn't make a noise, but when it spins the other way we get that.'

'Well, it sounds most uncanny,' Forbes remarked, sitting down opposite his hostess, i could have sworn you'd got some frightened child shut up in one of the attics.'

'Quite ghostly, isn't it?' Gladys laughed. 'We never believed in ghosts, but we thought at first we'd got one. We soon found out that it was the chimney-cowl, but it scared us at first.'

'You must have thought it was the ghost of one of the kids who were here when the house was a school?' Forbes suggested.

Husband and wife exchanged smiling glances.

'We never thought of that,' Telford said. 'What I call a nice, cheerful suggestion! Pity you weren't here to remind us the first time we heard it. It would have made going up to bed seem still more adventurous.'

For the moment Forbes was disinclined to let the subject drop.

'You hear it in the day, then?' he asked.

'Not to notice,' Telford returned indifferently. 'Plenty of other noises then. Besides, during the day one takes no notice of sounds which seem pretty ominous at night.'

When Forbes went up to bed the house was silent.

'Wind's dropped or changed again,' he remarked to Telford. But he was hardly in bed when the sobbing and crying, which now seemed to come from close overhead, broke out again. He lay listening, conscious of a vague uneasiness and a quicker beating of the heart, 'If that's a cowl,' he thought, 'I'll eat it.'

Presently he jumped out of bed, wetted his index-finger, and held his hand out in the night air. 'H'm!' he muttered, withdrawing his hand over the sash. 'Wind seems to be nor'-east. Ray was wrong.'

He stood irresolute a moment, cold and strangely uncomfortable.

'Still,' he thought, 'if it's a chimney-cowl it's a chimney-cowl, and that finishes it. And if they're satisfied, why shouldn't I be?'

He went back to bed, but he did not fall asleep until the sobbing noise had ceased and the house was quiet.

The following afternoon brought upon the scene Master Derek Wilson in the black coat and dark trousers which were the uniform of school servitude, and the customary 'going-away' bowler hat. He was a tall, dark, fresh-faced boy with a friendly grin and a very happy laugh. He brought with him two periodicals, one devoted to wireless and the other to motorcycling, and, after having been introduced to Forbes, followed his luggage upstairs to array himself in gorgeous tweeds. He came down again whistling, full of high spirits, and demanded to be allowed to explore. Telford was not yet home from the office, so Forbes accompanied him.

'Thank everything the bally spring term's over,' he remarked to Forbes.

'Hockey and Lent is a ghastly combination. Gladys looks fit. How's old Ray? Had an invite to go and stay with a chap in my house whose people live in Earl's Court, but I wanted to have a look at this stately home of England which Gladys and Ray have got hold of. Besides, there's nothing to do in London now, and you want such bags of money.'

'Which nobody seems to have nowadays,' Forbes remarked.

'Especially when you've got trustees,' Derek added cryptically.

On the whole, he struck Forbes as being quite a nice boy, who could be enthusiastic without gushing and seemed easy to please and entertain. He liked the house, and was glad that it contained no wireless set. He would put one up while he was there. He had never been in the New Forest before, and was glad of the opportunity to explore it. Forbes earned his gratitude by promising to take him around in his car while Telford was away at the office.

Indeed, the boy seemed perfectly happy in his surroundings and in the prospects held forth to him for the holidays.

Before going to bed that night he was warned about the chimney-cowl, but the peace of the house was not disturbed. Forbes, coming down early on the morning following, found Derek out on the drive talking to Robinson the old gardener. Derek greeted him with a grin and a wave of the hand.

'Robinson says this place used to be a school,' he said. 'Did you know?'

'I'd heard so. Must be pleasant for you to feel that you're still living in the odour of learning?'

'Oh, that must be near a 'undred years ago, sir,' said the literal Robinson.

'My gran'father used to tell me about it when I were a nipper. All sorts of stories 'e used to tell me. The man as kept the school used to starve the boys and beat 'em something 'orrible.'

'Good old Squeers!' laughed Derek, safe in his generation. 'That's the stuff to give 'em.'

'Well,' said Robinson seriously, 'as a matter of fact 'e were rather like that man Squeers as you reads about in Dickens, and this were just the same sort of school. There was no 'olidays, and people used to send boys 'ere just to get rid of 'em. Something bad 'appened at last—I never 'eard rightly what it was—and Ticks, the man 'oo kept the school, run away.'

'More than the boys could—with this wall around them,' commented Forbes. 'Derek, my lad, be thankful that you're twentieth-century vintage.'

The boy laughed.

'Oh, I wouldn't have stayed here with old Squeers,' he said, 'I'd have got away somehow, although it 'ud take a cat burglar to get out. And, talking of cat burglars, I believe old Robinson's one.'

'Me!' chuckled Robinson, who was sixty and rheumatic.

'Yes, you! What were you burying under the wall last night at the back of the house, at the kitchen garden end? Midnight, too! It looked suspicious.'

Robinson looked blank and Forbes chuckled.

'Robinson,' Forbes said, 'doesn't believe in working overtime.'

'Well, somebody was digging away like blazes. It wasn't you, and it wasn't Ray, because you'd just come up to bed. I was standing looking out of the window'

'Smoking, I s'pose?' interpolated Forbes.

'Ssh! Not a word to Ray! Anyhow, I was looking straight across the garden. You know what a fine bright night it was. There was hardly a breath of wind and everything was quite still, so that the sight of something moving caught my attention at once. It was a man digging away like steam at the foot of the wall close to the biggest pear-tree. I couldn't see him very clearly, but quite clearly enough to know what he was up to, and he was either burying something or digging something up. I thought it was a bit funny, and nearly went and told Ray. And then I thought it might be only somebody burying rubbish out of the kitchen, in which case I would look rather an ass, and you and Gladys and Ray would pull my leg about it all the hols. After a bit a cloud came up, and I couldn't see him anymore, so I waffled off to bed.'

Robinson was slightly up in arms. It was his garden, and he could not listen unmoved to this tale of unauthorised digging.

'Where did you say this was goin' on, sir?' he asked.

'Come along,' said Derek, 'and I'll show you. Dash! There goes the gong. Never mind. We've got time.'

He led the way around the side of the house, across the dewy lawn at the back, and on through the kitchen garden to the boundary wall.

'There you are,' he said, pointing, in that corner.'

Forbes and Robinson followed him and looked down. The crust of the earth was solid, hard, smooth, and stiffly knit. Robinson laughed.

'You been dreaming, young sir,' he said. 'That earth ain't been turned since I been 'ere, and you can see for yourself it weren't turned last night.'

The boy looked blank.

'But I swear' he began, and then broke off. 'Yes, it was here, too. It's the only part of the wall you can see from my window because of the trees. And I marked the place by this old pear-tree.'

Forbes laughed and punched him lightly on the shoulder.

'Come on to breakfast,' he said. 'You were dreaming.'

'I wasn't! I ought to know.'

'Well, if you weren't, you saw the shadows of the trees moving about. You and your cat burglars and people burying things at midnight! You'll be seeing ghosts next!'

During the day the incident was forgotten by all except Derek.

The next morning ushered in a torrent of rain which went thrashing through the leaves in the garden and beat upon the windows of the breakfast-room.

'I expected this,' said Telford, rubbing his hands. 'Heard our ghost again last night. That old chimney-cowl nearly always lets us know. Where's Derek?'

The maid who came in with the coffee-pot at that moment remarked that she thought Master Derek had gone out. She had been to his room with a cup of tea and found it empty and his clothes gone.

'He's gone for a walk in the Forest,' Telford remarked, 'and he's probably taking shelter somewhere out of the rain. Better keep something hot for him. It won't be much; only a heavy shower.'

But the clouds passed over and still no Derek appeared. Telford drove off to the office and, as time passed, Gladys Telford began to grow anxious.

Midday at last brought the second post, and, most surprisingly, a letter from Derek bearing the local postmark. Gladys opened it, frowned, and stared. Then she read the contents aloud to Forbes.

'Dear Gladys,
You'll think it horribly low-down of me for bunking off like this, but I can't help it. I don't want to tell you why I'm going—at least not yet. I'm catching the first train to London, and scribbling this note to you on the platform. I can't stay in your house another minute, so I'm off to stay with Lindley's people at Earl's Court. They asked me, so it will be quite all right. Don't think I'm a beast. I can't help doing this.
Love,
DEREK.

'Well, what on earth do you think of that?' Gladys exclaimed.

Forbes uttered a baffled laugh. 'It beats me. Why, only last night he was talking about going down to Hurst Castle, and I promised to run him down to Keyhaven in the car.'

'It's not a bit like Derek.'

'People,' said Forbes reflectively, when they leave a house in a hurry generally write a note there and then. Funny idea to write one on the station and post it. What time does the first train go?'

'Five o'clock. And the station's two and a half miles away. Why, the boy must have got up in the middle of the night. Look at the handwriting—how shaky it is.'

'The boy's been scared stiff by something,' Forbes almost said, but he looked at Gladys and checked himself in time.

'I wonder,' he said, rather unsteadily, 'if that chimney-cowl upset him.'

Gladys shook her head.

'We warned him what to expect. Besides, Derek wouldn't be such a baby.'

At that moment a maid appeared with a buff envelope on a salver, and inquired if there was an answer. The telegram was brief and to the point.

Derek arrived safely. Bringing him back to you tomorrow. LINDLEY.

'Well, that's that!' said Gladys. 'Poor Derek! I wonder what Ray will say about it?'

Telford said very little about it to his wife, but he was plainly very much annoyed. To have his hospitality slighted pricked him in his most vulnerable spot. Privately to Forbes he held forth long and sulphurously.

'Damned bad-mannered little beast! After all we've done for him! To go sneaking off like that. I'll never have him in the house again. When this Lindley brings him back I'll send him off somewhere for the rest of his holidays. I'm finished with him!'

Forbes had his own opinion about Derek's conduct, or, rather, vague and uncomfortable theories had begun to form in his mind. He, too, had heard those noises, so terribly like a child in an extremity of woe, on the preceding night.

The chimney-cowl? Was it? Could a chimney-cowl really produce sounds so completely and utterly human? Because the chimney-cowl certainly made noises at times, the Telfords and their servants, all hard-headed and practical folk, were completely satisfied that all sounds, otherwise unaccountable, proceeded from it.

He did not believe in manifestations of the supernatural, but his scepticism was not bigoted. The Telfords said in effect: 'There is no child in the house, there are no such things as ghosts, and therefore it must be the chimney-cowl.' Forbes did not go all the way with them. Apparently nobody had gone up to the attics in the dark to make sure, unless - Here came a thought which set his nerves tingling unpleasantly and strangely chilled him. Nobody had gone to investigate, unless Derek had.

Forbes could not help remembering that the house had once been used as a school by a scoundrel who starved and ill-treated unwanted and friendless children. In his walled-in house in the New Forest he had been as immune from observation as the Yorkshire schoolmasters whom Dickens pilloried. At last there had been a scandal and the man had run away. What scandal? It was buried now in the limbo of lost things, whence, in all human probability, it would never be dug up again. But certain it was that the walls of this sad old house had once heard the cries and sobs of maltreated children which now the chimney-cowl—was it the chimney-cowl?—so strangely imitated.

But he said nothing to the Telfords. They would have laughed at him or heard him not too patiently. The following day, Good Friday, would bring Derek back, doubtless with a tale which would confirm or disprove the unpleasant suspicions which were taking doubtful shape in his imagination. That night Forbes slept soundly for an hour or two, and then woke for no reason that he could guess. The sounds which he heard faintly and seemed to be proceeding from the floor above—sounds like the moaning and crying of a child—were not loud enough to have wakened him. But now that he was awake he lay listening, while awe and fear struggled with a rising sense of shame.

He wanted to investigate, and wanted not to. Courage urged him on, fear held him back, and shame looked on and sneered.

Derek had dared to go up to those attics. He was almost sure now that Derek had gone. Derek was a boy, he a man, and he was holding back.

Shame stung him to activity at last. He cursed himself, got out of bed, felt for dressing-gown and slippers, and shuffled out on to the landing.

The staircase leading to the attics was a narrow, straight, steep flight. There was no window on the top landing, and the stairhead was lost in darkness. Somewhere quite close a child sobbed and moaned, and, while his heart gave a warning of the tighter hold of fear, he could have sworn that it was a human voice.

It was not until he faced the wall of darkness above him that he realised that he had neglected to bring candle or matches. He shook the pocket of his dressing-gown in vain. He hesitated, realising that if he went back to his room to procure a light his resolution would waver and desert him. Slowly he mounted the stairs—one, two, three, four of them. Then the sobbing became a muffled wail which died into silence, and he looked up.

Something moved in the darkness at the top of the stairs. It seemed suddenly to be pierced by a faint light, as the moon is sometimes seen looking through murky clouds not dense enough to hide it. While every nerve cried out upon the outrage thus done to his senses he beheld the figure of a man about to descend.

He did not notice what clothes the Thing appeared to wear, although he will carry to his grave the memory of the thin, attenuated hands. But it was the face which visited all his subsequent bad dreams—a face almost grotesquely evil, long and livid, and splashed across the right cheek with a hideous red discoloration of the skin. The eyes were small, closely set, and smouldered as if with some evil fire. The knowledge—the certain knowledge—that he was faced with something not of this world was sufficient to drive Forbes to an extremity of terror, but it was the indescribable vileness of the Thing which momentarily bereft him of his wits and atrophied all his nerves of motion.

Agony drew out time, spending it like a miser. Whole minutes while the descending feet passed from stair to stair. Somewhere, deep down in Forbes's tortured brain, the machinery still worked. The Thing was descending and would pass him—would pass him on stairs so narrow that one human being could scarcely crowd past another. The prospect of close proximity, of actual touch, gave him another push along the road leading to madness. He struggled to move as one in a nightmare struggles to wake. Mercifully, something seemed to snap, leaving him free to spring backwards, to sprawl and plunge at the foot of the stairs, and thence to rush for his bedroom, where he turned on the friendly electric light before pressing his face into his pillow.

It is not necessary to this account to describe how he spent what remained of that long night. He came down in the morning looking the sick man that he felt himself to be. The Telfords asked him what was the matter, and, strangely, he felt that he could not tell them. Drearily he felt that he did not know how to begin to tell them. He could now only wait for Derek.

Derek arrived at three in the afternoon, white-faced, after a drive of a hundred miles through crisp, spring weather in an open car. He came accompanied by a grey, dapper, middle-aged man, who gave his name as Colonel Lindley.

'I expect you've heard of me?' he said to Telford with a faint smile.

'My boy and Derek are friends at school. I invited Derek to spend the Easter holidays with us, but found that you had forestalled me. I should be very glad to have him, but I did not like the way he had left you without any explanation, so I have brought him back to tell you his story like a man.'

Telford was looking at the boy in no friendly way; and Derek, white and fidgeting, kept his gaze bent downwards.

'If,' continued Colonel Lindley, with a tactful glance at Gladys, 'Derek and I could have a word with you alone '

'I don't think that's at all necessary, Colonel Lindley. My wife is his sister. Derek can have nothing to complain of in the way he has been treated here.'

'Certainly not. But I was thinking that if Mrs Telford were nervous - To put it bluntly, the fact is that Derek thinks he's seen a ghost.'

Derek looked up at the faint sound of derision which came from his brother-in-law's lips. The boy's eyes suddenly flashed.

'Yes, you dare to laugh!' he cried. 'You go through what I went through and then see if you laugh!'

'There, old chap!' said the colonel, and touched his arm. 'Mr Telford,' he continued, 'whatever you and I may believe on the subject of apparitions, and whatever the explanation may be, it is quite evident that poor old Derek has had a bad shock. His nerves are all to pieces. Aren't they, old man? I know you would not wish to keep with you a boy who is badly scared of the house, and I trust I was not officious in promising that he should return with me.

Meanwhile, he owes you an explanation. Apart from that, I think you will agree that there are reasons why you should hear his story.'

The pinched, white face of the boy touched Telford in spite of himself.

'Well, what did you see, Derek?' he asked, not unkindly.

For the moment it looked as if Derek were about to cry.

'I can't,' he muttered, with a queer, half-hysterical petulance. 'I can't talk about it! '

Forbes drew nearer to the boy.

'Never mind, old man,' he said unsteadily. 'They'll believe you. I saw him, too.'

For the moment every pair of eyes were on Forbes. Telford uttered an exclamation and a faint cry came from Derek.

'You!' he gasped. 'You've seen him? What—the little boy?'

'No; the man.'

The boy struggled and choked.

'Oh, he was worse! It was him that finished me. Did you see that red mark on his face? A port wine mark they call it, don't they? Tell them you saw that, and then they'll believe'

'I saw it,' said Forbes unsteadily, 'and I'm not likely to forget it.'

'Good Lord!' said Telford, just above his breath.

Derek drew a deep breath and seemed to gain courage,

'I'll try to tell you what happened,' he said. 'You'll remember I didn't go to bed until you did the night before last. And when I got to my room there was a book I wanted to finish, so I sat up reading for about an hour. I'd only just got into bed when I heard that dreadful crying noise which you said was the chimney-cowl.' He paused and swallowed. 'Well, it wasn't!' he added laconically. 'Where was I? Oh, yes, I know! I lay and listened, and the more I listened the more I felt sure that it wasn't the chimney-cowl. I somehow felt that there was a kid in one of those attics, and I had to go and see. A real kid, I thought it was. I swear I never thought about ghosts.

'Well, I got to the top of the attic stairs, and the sound seemed to come from the room at the end. It was pitch dark, and I had to feel my way along. In the dark I tumbled against a door and pushed it open, and then—I don't know why I didn't faint, but I just stood still and felt as if I were dead.

'The room was just light—a faint greenish light it was, and I don't know where it came from. It was quite bare except for a table and a chair. On the chair before the table there was a boy, sitting. He looked about twelve or thirteen, and he was dressed like a kid in those old pictures of Dickens's stories—only he was dirty and ragged and his hair was rather long. He was crying terribly and his eyes were all swollen. He looked up at me once, and I shall never forget the look in his eyes. Then he went on writing.

'I forgot to tell you he was writing something. I can't tell you everything at once, just as I saw it. There were one or two mouldy old books on the table and some bits of paper, and the boy was writing with one of those old quill pens—an ordinary white feather.

'I knew he wasn't real—I mean real like ourselves—but I tried to talk to him and found I couldn't say a word. Presently, when he'd finished writing, he looked at me again as if he wanted something. Then he got up, still crying and moaning, and went over to the window and slipped the piece of paper he'd been writing on through a crack in the window-seat. It must have been a very narrow crack, for the paper kept on bending and he had to tease it through. And all the time he kept on looking round at me as if to make sure that I was watching him.

'When he'd done, he came away from the window-seat, still looking at me, and suddenly his face changed. Before I could wonder why, something brushed past me. It was a tall, thin man in black—oh, a horrible beast—with a great red mark on his cheek. He was carrying a thick stick, and he made a rush straight at the boy. I heard the boy scream. Then, I suppose, I must have fainted, for I woke up presently on the bare floor, and the room was all dark.

'I don't remember getting back to my bedroom. I think I must have jumped or fallen downstairs, for I found myself bruised all over. The only thing I could think of was getting out of the house. I didn't even want you, Ray, or Gladys. You couldn't have helped, and you'd have kept me talking, and you mightn't have let me go, and then I should have gone mad. I had to get straight out of the house or go mad. I gathered my clothes up in a bundle and put them on in the front drive. I'd forgotten my tie, and I found I'd left a sock behind, but I didn't care. I wasn't going back for them. I bought a tie and a pair of socks in London before going on to Colonel Lindley's. I walked to the station and found it all shut up, but I climbed the railings and sat on the platform until the first train came in. The booking-clerk, when he came, gave me a bit of paper and an envelope and sold me a stamp, so I wrote to Gladys, but it was no use trying to say what had happened. You must have thought me an awful beast, but I couldn't help it. And I'm going back with Colonel Lindley, if you don't mind. I'd rather die than sleep another night here.'

Derek came abruptly to the end of his story, and looked up gratefully into Forbes's face, as Forbes laid a steadying hand on his shoulder. Nobody spoke at first. In the face of that story, which seemed so incredible and yet rang so true, nothing could have been said which would not have sounded ridiculously inadequate. Telford was the first to speak.

'I think we'll take a look at that attic," he said gruffly.

'I'm not coming with you!' Derek cried out.

'AH right, old chap,' his brother-in-law said soothingly. 'The attic at the end, you said?'

'At the end on the left,' muttered the boy.

'Right! Colonel Lindley'

'I should like to come with you, if I may,' the Colonel replied simply.

Gladys put her arm around her brother. The hand which patted his shoulder shook a little. 'You stay down here with me, old thing,' she said.

Telford led the way upstairs, and it was he who pushed open the attic door.

'This must be the one,' he said. 'H'm! No table or chair here, you see. I knew there wasn't.'

'I didn't expect to see any,' Forbes remarked dryly.

The room was bare save for the dust which rose up chokingly from the boards under their feet. In the empty shell of the room their voices sounded strange and hollow.

Colonel Lindley walked over to the window.

'There's certainly a window-seat,' he remarked, 'and there are plenty of cracks in it.'

Telford followed, and laid his hand on the surface of the seat.

'I suppose we'd better have this off,' he said, 'I'll go down and get some tools from the kitchen.'

'You'll have to smash it,' said Forbes. 'Get an axe.'

Telford left them and went downstairs. He returned presently with tools, including an axe, and it was the axe which eventually did the work of destruction.

The box-like space underneath was full of the dust and debris of ages.

Splinters and scraps of mortar had found their way there. Forbes pulled the rubbish out in handfuls, and exclaimed suddenly on seeing a dirty and discoloured scrap of paper. He held it to the light, gently stroking the dirt away with his thumbs.

The removal of the dirt showed faint, pink, ruled lines which served to show that the paper had once been torn from an account-book or exercise-book. On it something was written in faded black ink. The writing was round and childish, but so faint that it was not easy to decipher. The three men bent over it, picking out words and slowly stringing them together. The writing was in the form of a statement. Punctuated and with the spelling amended, it was as follows:

I have been locked in this room for a punishment five days and five nights. Mr Hicks comes and beats me something cruel. I think he means to kill me. I think my uncle wants me to be dead. If I die here nobody will ever know, because Mr Cawland, the usher, is as bad as Mr Hicks, and they will tell the boys that I have been sent away. So I have written this down and I am going to put it through a crack in the window-ledge, so as perhaps it will be found some day, and then people will know all about it.
(Signed) JOHN THIRKHILL.

The three men looked at one another. For a little while there was only the sound of breathing.

Telford still struggled not to believe. 'Is this a hoax, or what is it?' he said presently, as if to himself, I mean—a boy might easily write such a statement, without any real cause. And when he was let out at the end of the punishment he wouldn't be able to recover this scrap of paper from the place where we found it.'

Forbes made an impatient gesture.

'In the face of what Derek has told us,' he began, 'there seems to be only'

'I know. It's incredible, but it seems almost conclusive. What do you think, Colonel Lindley?'

'I think it's murder most foul. We must inform the police'

'Murder most foul in the eighteen-thirties or thereabouts,' Forbes interrupted gently. 'Too late now, Hicks'—he shuddered—'Hicks has gone to his own place long since. No man can avenge little John Thirkhill now.'

Telford passed a hand over his damp brow.

'I feel queer and sick,' he said. 'I didn't believe . . . There's nothing we can do now, then? Except get out of this accursed house. Nothing else we can do?'

'Yes,' said Forbes gently, 'there's just one thing. Perhaps when we've done that we shan't hear—your chimney-cowl—anymore.'

'Ah!' exclaimed Telford, and flinched.

'Your gardener isn't about, is he?'

'No, he gets a day off. He may be down at the lodge or he may not.

Why?'

'It doesn't matter. I want some garden tools—just a spade and a pick. Don't you remember Derek looked out of his window one night and said he saw somebody digging. I know the spot because he took me there.'

Derek heard the three men leave the house.

'Where are they going?' he asked.

'I don't know.' Gladys's arm was still about his shoulders. 'I don't expect they'll be long. Don't worry, old thing.'

She felt a tremor go through him.

'I know,' he said, with a sudden intuition. 'They're going out to dig.

They're going to dig in the garden.'

They were not very long gone. The earth was soft, and they found what they sought four feet below the surface. They came back silent and white and grave, and none looked straight into Derek's face.

'Have you—have you found anything?' the boy asked jerkily.

'We'll tell you—all about it—someday, old man,' Telford stammered.

'Yes, don't tell me—yet.'

The boy crossed over to Colonel Lindley, touched his arm, and looked up piteously into his face.

'Are you ready to go now, Colonel Lindley?' he asked.

At The Toy Mender's

Old Pere Petard earned a precarious, and probably insufficient, living by mending toys. In every town there are one or two who invent or improvise a means of livelihood undreamed of by most of their fellow men and women. Old Petard was one of these; and even when times were at their hardest he could rest secure in the knowledge that he had no local rivals in business.

He was very, very old. How old nobody could exactly say, but grey-haired men and women remembered him when they were children, and swore that he looked as old then as now. Age, however, had not destroyed his skill. The children of this generation found him as adept at restoring the lost eye of a wax doll, or making a rickety lead soldier stand firmly upright, as ever their parents did.

Lucille made his acquaintance at a very early age, and she afterwards remembered him for having paid her what she considered to be her first real compliment. In those days she had a beautiful doll dressed as a Zouave soldier, with baggy red breeches and a long, curled moustache which few female hearts could have withstood. Him she loved dearly, and as he was for ever suffering injuries—as, indeed, befitted a soldier—she was for ever bringing him to the alley off the town square, down the two steps, and through the low doorway which gave entrance to Pere Petard's workshop. And for a two sous piece at the most she received him back, if not as good as new, at least presentable and fit to be nursed.

But there came a day when Lucille, still a child, brought to old Petard a new doll gorgeously arrayed as a naval officer, such a doll as a rich man's child might covet. Old Petard opened his blear eyes wide upon it.

'Eh, eh,' he exclaimed, 'what a fine toy! And new! What is the matter with the sailor, Lucille?'

'There is nothing the matter with him, Pere Petard,' she answered. 'I have brought him to make you acquainted. Is he not beautiful?'

The old man admired him while he fingered a stick of solder.

'And what of the Zouave?'

'Oh! Pierre?' She gave a little grown-up shrug of the shoulders to denote that she had finished with him. 'It is Jacques that I love now.' She held her new love close against her cheek and smiled at the old man through the doll's hair. 'An English gentleman, a stranger, gave him to me, because my eyes are so blue and my hair so glossy, and because the sound of my laughter pleased him. I chose Jacques out of a hundred at the great shop.'

The old man adjusted his spectacles to his comfort and regarded her. He had known many generations of children and watched them grow up. They lived around him now, honest and thieving, straight and crooked, scholars, courtesans, priests, and matrons. None knew better than he of what manner of man a child was likely to be father.

'You are but a doll yourself, little one,' he said.

Now Lucille clapped her hands and laughed, for to look like a girl-doll was one of her ambitions. She achieved her ambition in more than mere looks, for she had such brains as a doll might have if God breathed life into it, and the blood in her veins was seldom warmer than sawdust.

'Take heed,' said the old man, 'lest some day you come to me broken. For I cannot mend you.'

She laughed at that, as she was ever afterwards wont to laugh at warnings, and hugged to herself the old man's remark about her being like a doll. Afterwards in her home she postured before a great mirror, and admired the forget-me-not blue of her own eyes and the wave of her yellow hair. She was eleven years old at the time.

When Lucille was seventeen her parents began to try to arrange a marriage for her, first with a baker and then with a young doctor. But they were weak folk, and Lucille's waywardness defeated them. She herself had nothing but scorn for the provincial bourgeoisie among whom she had been reared. She had seen people who came from another world, haughty and magnificent folk who came to drink the waters and play in the Casino, representatives of great commercial houses in Paris and Lyons who seemed not to be of the common clay.

Such men as looked about them for adventures found Lucille ready to meet them half way. She was hunting big game, but intending to select carefully before she cast her net. Soon she was known as a *cocotte,* and half-envied, half-despised by the other and plainer girls who knew her. Malice vented itself in laughter and prophecies of disaster. 'She will make a *betise*, that one, you will see.' 'That Lucille will not make a good end.'

Lucille was apparently indifferent to all the criticism she evoked; secretly she revelled in it. There are those to whom notoriety is a necessary condiment of life. So, still disdaining the lights of the common earth around her, she spread moth's wings towards the stars.

One day she saw old Petard, bent to the shape of a note of interrogation, shuffling across the square towards his alley with a long brown loaf under his arm. It was the first time they had seen each other since she was a child. She was brave in Parisian finery, the gift of her latest admirer, and spread out her skirt before the old man as a butterfly spreads wings.

'And am I still like a doll, Pere Petard?' she asked.

'Still like a doll,' he repeated. 'Take heed! I cannot mend such dolls as you once they are broken.'

She frowned and pouted.

'Still mending toys, Pere Petard?' she asked. 'Still working as hard as ever?'

'Sometimes far into the night,' he answered. 'The toys of today are more easily broken and harder to mend. There is more work, and I am slower than I once was.'

She watched him shuffle into the alley like a lamed wild animal into its hole, wondering what joy the old man had of life, why he had lived so long, what choice or chance had made him the servant of generation after generation of children. But she did not ponder long. She never wasted much thought on anything which did not concern herself.

There came to the town one Raoul Montard, a young man of fashion and apparent means, who announced himself to be the son of a banker. He frequented the Casino and played baccarat recklessly, and with that good luck which sometimes attends the reckless. Him Lucille took for her lover, and afterwards set her scheming little head to work. This to some purpose, as you shall find.

At fall of dusk on an evening in early spring she met Montard on the steps of the Casino, and as they turned in the direction of the cafe where dinner had been ordered, she asked him what fortune.

'I won twelve thousand francs,' he said, 'and lost two thousand back. The luck turned, and so I left.'

Lucille laughed and clapped her little gloved hands.

'Ten thousand francs!' she exclaimed. 'But that is magnificent—five thousand francs each.'

He was humming an air which the Casino band had been playing, and now glanced at her with a sidelong smile.

'Are we then partners, my little one?' he demanded.

Lucille nodded. 'Could it be a better partnership?' she asked. 'You are clever; I have chic, and I am no fool. Besides, my Raoul, when the police are looking for one, it is better to have a partner than an enemy.'

Montard went on humming. He emitted only one false note, and then quickly recovered himself. Lucille heard it, and smiled sidelong at him. She had him so securely in the hollow of her hand.

'When you take off your coat, stupid one,' she said, 'it is possible to read what letters are in your pockets if you leave them there.'

Montard shrugged and smiled and went on humming. Behind the good-humoured mask on his face he was thinking hard. Lucille was very well, but a partnership is an embarrassment to a gentleman of fortune who prefers to remain unfettered.

'So,' said Lucille blithely, 'we are partners, eh?'

Montard stopped humming to reply: 'If you say it, my clever little one.'

They were now in the town square, and she laid a hand on his arm and made him stop.

'If we go this way,' she said, pointing to the mouth of the alley in which lived the old toy mender, 'we cut a great corner. We also pass the shop of old Pere Petard, who used to mend my dolls when I was a child.'

They entered the dark alley side by side, and Lucille continued:

'He is very, very old and a great fool. He has been mending toys all his life. He mended them for my grandparents, and talked in their day, as he talks now, like a copybook of maxims. I do not doubt that when I am under the ground he will be still there, mending toys.'

As a great hand with fingers of steel suddenly clapped over Lucille's mouth, she heard Montard's voice say:

'That is very possible.'

There is always one way of dissolving a partnership. Theirs was dissolved by the long knife which went home with a soft thud between Lucille's shoulder-blades.

Old Petard, toiling slowly in his shop, was startled by the sound of something tumbling down the two steps and striking the door. It gave way beneath the weight, and something pitched into the room, oversetting a small table on which a number of damaged toys awaited his surgery.

The old man started up with a little cry, and his spectacles jogged half an inch from the red mark across the bridge of his nose.

When he adjusted them again he saw Lucille lying among the other broken toys on the floor of the shop.

The Little Blue Flames

Ferrers had been looking at the brass candlesticks for some time. Presently he rose, took them from my sitting-room mantelpiece, and held them in his hands appraisingly as if he were trying to guess their weight. He closed his eyes for a moment and frowned.

'Where did you get these?' he asked.

'Oh, I came by them honestly!' I laughed, 'I bought them at a second-hand shop. Why?'

'You don't know anything about their history?'

'One doesn't ask for the pedigree of almost worthless second-hand articles. They're of no intrinsic value, a bit battered, and not old enough to be called antiques. But I'm fond of brass, and I happened to like their shape. You apparently don't.'

'I don't object to their shape,' said Ferrers, 'but I don't like them. To me there's something repellent in the sight of them, much more in the touch.

They've been connected with something ghastly.'

He put them back with a theatrical air of haste and wiped his perfectly clean fingers on his coat.

Ferrers was a very good fellow, but a bit of a crank and, I was sure, more than a bit of a charlatan. We were office mates. Like most cranks he played chess rather well, and although I believed myself to be fairly normal, I, too, played a pretty good game. Thus we often came to visit each other's rooms of an evening.

Ferrers was of the type much beloved of middle-aged, superstitious women. You know those dear ladies who have outgrown a faith which has supported millions during the past two thousand years, but can still believe that their futures can be ascertained by shaking up the dregs in a teacup.

'Dear Mr Ferrers is so clever! He is ever so psychic and susceptible to "atmospheres", but not quite a clairvoyant, my dear, because he will not develop his wonderful gift.' Ferrers was taken about and exhibited at quite a lot of tea-parties.

When he was taken to a house three or four hundred years old he generally had some shuddersome things to say about it. A tragedy had happened there. He couldn't say what it was, but there was a sinister atmosphere in one of the rooms. And since nobody could contradict him everybody accepted his word, and was impressed by his remarkable gift.

If on the other hand he went to a house which he knew had been specially built by the happy young married couple who still inhabited it he looked just as wise and discoursed on the benevolence of the atmosphere.

Nothing tragic had ever happened there! Clever Mr Ferrers! For those who care to try it this is the simplest way in the world of getting kudos and free meals.

Please note the simplicity of his methods. He had first noticed that my candlesticks were fairly old and rather battered. After that he had ascertained from my own lips that I knew' nothing of their history. All then was plain sailing. He 'sensed' something sinister about them, and although I might laugh at him I could not disprove his statement.

I did laugh at him.

'I've been lying to you,' I said. 'Those candlesticks were standing on a table in the room at Holyrood when Rizzio was murdered. Afterwards they came south to England, and provided the light by which Sir Edmondbury Godfrey was murdered. Afterwards they passed into the possession of Thurtell, the murderer of Weir. I forget how many other murders they've been connected with. They seem to cause murder. Very likely they will make me murder you. Have a drink, Ferrers.'

He smiled at me as a man will when he dismisses a weak joke, if I were you,' he said, 'I should get rid of them—sell them, or give them away, and get another pair.'

'What'll you give me for them? They're only worth a shilling or two.'

'Oh, I don't want them! I wouldn't live with them for anything!'

'Come off it!' I laughed. 'You're not in good psychic form tonight otherwise you wouldn't have lost the game, when you had it well in hand, by letting me take your queen.'

'It was those darned things,' Ferrers said, pointing to the mantelpiece. 'I couldn't keep my mind off them.'

'You've met them before,' I said mildly. 'They've been here for months, but they haven't worried you until tonight.'

'I know,' he answered, i don't pretend to understand it. There are no discovered laws about these things. Perhaps it is only at certain seasons of the year that they become repulsive to a sensitive like myself. Probably you're quite safe with them. If you've got a brick instead of a head you can't expect to feel much.'

I swallowed the jibe. I could always get my own back on Ferrers, the deluder of old maids who were always having their fortunes told, and were not in the least deterred by the fact that they came out different every time. I mixed him a drink, sat on chatting with him for another quarter of an hour, and then verbally turfed him out by telling him that I was jolly well going to bed.   But quite unconsciously I was affected by Ferrers's words. You know how it is when you meet a man and like him, and then somebody comes and warns you against him, whispering in your ear a word or two of unpleasant scandal. You may not believe it, but you haven't quite the same ease in his company afterwards. So it was with me and my candlesticks. Ferrers had uttered the poisoned word, and for two or three days afterwards I found myself disliking them and nearly following his advice. Then I forgot all about it.

It happened that about three weeks later I shuffled my household goods.

Those who live, or have lived, in two rooms understand the deadly monotony of that sort of existence. You get sick of the sight of your small possessions. The best way to overcome that is to move them about—shift the bookcase from one wall to another, turn the table so that its long ends are where its flanks used to be, find new places for the pictures and ornaments.

Thus it happened that the battered, old brass candlesticks came to occupy positions on either side of my bedroom mantelpiece.

My bedroom was on the second floor and the one large window looked out across a street in Bloomsbury on the sooty facade of another house similar to the one in which I lodged. The window was flanked by the inevitable dirty 'lace' curtains, looped towards the lower ends and bearing the design of a shepherd boy surrounded by impossible flowers piping to invisible sheep.

My bed pointed straight at this window, the head of it lying flush with the opposite wall. There was a space on either side. The door was at my right hand when I lay on my back. The fireplace and mantelpiece were in the middle of the left-hand wall. Here my candlesticks rested, and on those mornings when the sun happened to be shining I could see the gleam of their brass by looking slightly to my left across the foot of the bed. These details of my bedroom are as necessary as they may be tiresome.

I never had candles in the sticks. I had both gas and electric light, obtainable through little boxes clamped to the floor which were always hungry for shillings at inconvenient moments. The candlesticks were merely articles of decoration and not of utility.

Most nights I went to bed early, but occasionally I went to a theatre and had a late meal afterwards. Late suppers never agreed with me and it was on those nights that I slept worst. It was on the occasion when I had been to see Journey's End and taken a hurried meal afterwards—including lobster—that the first and lesser of my two unpleasant experiences befell me.

I want to be quite impartial, stating all the facts, and that is why I confess to the lobster.

I got into bed at about half-past twelve, having first turned out the electric light. The switch was by the door and out of reach from the bed. It was a black night, and while I undressed I heard the steady whirr of the expected rain on the road outside and a gurgling and choking of water running into gutters. The window was just a pale rectangle and I could hardly discern any of the bedroom furniture.

The lobster has his own way of taking revenge on mankind. The poor devil is plunged alive into boiling water. He therefore gets his own back on those who eat him. Mine arranged for me many sleepless hours. I kept my eyes resolutely closed, lay on my right side, and waited for sleep in vain. I heard the London clocks striking every quarter of an hour, the sonorous voice of Big Ben deepening or softening his tone at the wind's will. And still the rain droned and pattered outside, and still I could not sleep.

After a long while I turned over and opened my eyes. The best thing, it seemed to me, was to jump out, turn on the light, and go and fetch a book. But when I opened my eyes I was astonished to see that a dim light already pervaded the room.

It was not moonlight. Besides, there could be no moon with that drenching downpour still going on. Nor could the light have come from the opposite window across the street, for my own window looked darker than ever. I was idly curious at first. There was no smell of burning, nothing at which to take alarm. The light was very dim and bluish. Although the window was dark it must surely, I thought, be reflected into the room from outside.

And then I looked straight over at the mantelpiece and gasped.

Flickering just over the tops of my two brass candlesticks were two little blue flames. There were no candles in the sticks: indeed, so far as I knew there was not a candle in the house. These small flames seemed to be feeding on nothing, to have independent lives, to be hovering in the air like little phosphorescent moths. You know when sometimes you light a new candle and it seems uncertain for a few moments if the candle will burn. The little weak flame you see then is just like the flames I stared at from my bed.

To me—since I knew they could not be candle-flames—the oddest thing was that they were poised just above the candlesticks. Of course, it was a reflection, some sort of optical illusion, and the obvious step to take was to jump out of bed and walk across to take a closer view. It was only when I moved a leg, preparatory to doing so, that I found myself powerless. Fear leaped upon me like a wild beast out of a thicket. It was an inexplicable panic terror of which I was afterwards thoroughly ashamed, but which at the time I was powerless to combat.

In the midst of this sudden and wild galloping brain-storm I remembered what Ferrers had said about the candlesticks. There was something sinister and uncanny about them. And I knew with a certainty—which had grown, like my dread, out of nothing—that if I lay and watched I should see something unbearable. I did what I had so often done as a little frightened child when I woke in the night and thought I heard some strange noise in the dark. I plunged down into the bed and drew the clothes right over me. I lay in mental torture for a period which threatened eternity. Once I thought I heard a scuffling in the room close to the foot of my bed. Then I suppose I must have fallen asleep, for I returned to consciousness when I heard a teacup rattling in its saucer close to my ear and the familiar friendly sound of my landlady's voice.

'Oh, Mr Roberts! Fancy! It's a wonder you didn't die of suffocation.'

It was a man with a headache and very little pride who got out of bed a few minutes later. What was I to think? Had any other man told me the experience which I have just described I should have laughed at him. I should have said: 'This charlatan Ferrers tells you some rot about those candlesticks, and eventually you get a bad dream about them after a lobster supper.' It was the feasible and only reasonable explanation, but such explanations, while they're always applicable to the other fellow, are no good to ourselves. Because it had happened to me, I couldn't convince myself that it was a dream.

I carried the memory of it all day like a burden, but the burden lightened as the day drew on. My work in the office lightened it, for one cannot concentrate one's mind on two things at once. By the evening I had decided that my last night's experience was just 'queer', but capable of some absurdly simple explanation. My sudden terror was induced by the memory of what Ferrers had said.

That evening I went round to Ferrers's rooms to play chess, but I said nothing to him about the previous night. It would have been a score for him and also it might have tempted him to enlarge on the subject to such an extent as to give me another beastly dream. I returned to my rooms at about midnight, entered my bedroom, and, walking about while I took off my collar and tie, I suddenly found myself confronting the two brass candlesticks.

The obvious thing to do, to insure against a recurrence of what had happened last night, was to dump them in the sitting-room. I had almost seized one of them, when I drew back. That would be cowardly. I had not yet recovered from the shame of my last night's fear, and I knew that the way to breed terror was to make concessions to it. What I had seen last night was capable of some simple explanation, and my fear had bubbled out of my subconscious mind for reasons already stated. Here was I, sane and sound and healthy, and what had I to fear from a pair of brass candlesticks? Put them back in my sitting-room? Certainly not! They must stay in my bedroom and I must teach myself that what I dreamed or imagined last night was nonsense. It was that idiot Ferrers who dropped the germ into my mind. Let all his bogies come and do their worst—if they existed.

Eventually I switched off the electric light, jumped into bed, and was soon asleep.

I don't know what woke me, but when I did wake the room was once more illumined. I did not at once think about the candlesticks, for I had all the hazy feelings of one who becomes half-awake in a strange room. I began to ask myself where on earth I could be.

To begin with, the door was in the wrong place. It should have been at the end of the wall close to my right hand. Now it was diagonally opposite, set in the far corner of the left-hand wall and close to the window. It was standing wide open, so wide that it formed an acute angle with the wall. This was very odd!

Another odd thing was a change which had taken place in the window. It used to be high and narrow, now it was long and low. It used to be flanked by not too clean lace curtains. Now it wore a veil of pink-muslin, hanging down from brass rings along a curtain pole at the top.

Between my bed-rail and the window there was a table, laid for a meal.

A woman stood with her back to me and seemed to be preparing food. She was poorly dressed and after a fashion which died before I was born. She wore a blouse, and a belt around her waist, and the hem of the blouse lay around her hips like a soldier's tunic.

My gaze travelled to the fireplace. It had become an open hearth with a log fire burning on it and a kettle stood suspended from a chain. On the high mantel stood several tawdry cottage ornaments—and my two brass candlesticks. There were candles in them now, bunting faint and blue, but they brightened even as I watched, and these, together with the firelight, illumined the room.

I stirred, mystified, but as yet not fully awake. How had I got to bed in some country cottage? Where was I, anyhow? Yet the bed was familiar, indeed the bed was mine. And those candlesticks.....

Then I began to remember. I had certainly gone to bed in my own room.

Had I not been playing chess with Ferrers? Then what had happened, and who was this woman, and how had the room beyond my bed-rail become so changed?

I knew that I was not dreaming. In dreams one loses all one's critical faculty. The most impossible and incredible things happen without causing the least surprise. But my critical faculty was not lost. It was arguing passionately against the evidence of my senses. Still, I must own that when I tried to speak I found that I had no voice.

And then fear leaped upon me again. I knew that something unspeakable was about to happen. Some remorseless Power had decreed that this time I was to endure the whole horror of it, and my gaze was forced in the direction of the open door.

The door had thrown a black shadow on the wall, and in this dark angle I was aware of something crouching. I saw the gleam of a long knife, and once more I tried to cry out, to move, to do something to warn that woman whose back was towards me; but only a convulsion seized me, and the sweat poured from me.

I seemed to know already what must happen. The woman was not preparing the meal for herself. When all was ready she would blow out those candles, preparatory to retiring for the night. And then—oh, I knew what was going to happen then.

There was something particularly ghastly to me in the leisured movements of the woman. I wanted to shriek out to her, like a yokel at a melodrama who sees the villain about to pounce on the heroine. But could I have shrieked I knew that it would make no difference, for the tragedy I was watching did not belong to the present. It had all happened so very long ago.

Presently she stood upright and, still half turned from me, moved across to the fireplace. I never saw her face. She picked up each candle in turn and out it went, and now the room was lit only by the flickering blood-red glow of the fire.

I heard the door swing and close with a crash. Something leaped from behind it into the firelight. There was a scream and a snarl and a mad mingling and leaping of shadows. Then I fainted.

When I awoke in the morning my room was normal, and the brass candlesticks beamed innocently at me in the pallid sunlight of a half-hearted dawn.

Of course, I told Ferrers about it. He affected to understand these things, and I began to think that he was not such a charlatan after all. He began by making that particularly irritating remark: 'Told you so.'

'But what do you make of it?' I asked.

'I know as much as you do,' he replied, 'and I doubt if either of us will ever know any more. You're not likely to find out much about a cottage tragedy of the 'seventies or 'eighties. Such things were common enough and always will be.'

'Influences sometimes cling to rooms, houses, country lanes, areas of open space; sometimes they cling to inanimate objects. I told you I didn't like your candlesticks. I should get rid of them if I were you.'

'I have,' I told him promptly.

'What have you done with them?' he asked.

'Chucked them into the dust-bin, and I didn't like even carrying them downstairs in broad daylight.'

'You should have slung them into the river,' Ferrers said.

Well, they've gone now, and I hope they were destroyed. But if the dustmen picked them out and sold them, I am afraid that there is a chance that somebody else may have a very uncomfortable time.

The Ticking Of The Clock

Hebden showed me to my room, and crossed it to pull the chintz curtains wider and thus give me the full benefit of the view across the water meadows. It was seven o'clock by summer-time, the sun was still fairly high, and the inhabitants of the rookery at the end of the garden had not yet thought of returning home.

The room was unpretentious but comfortable, and although it contained little besides necessities it had none of the uncompromising inhospitality of a hotel bedroom. There was, for instance, a table on the right-hand side of the bed which bore an assortment of the right kind of bedside books, such as Pepys's Diary, Chaucer's poems, and some of the works of Pater, Henry James, Meredith, and Stevenson. Hebden was not one of those people who thought that cheap and nasty pictures and ornaments were better than none at all. The mantelpiece was bare save for one article, and that was an article of utility.

I have called it an article of utility, for so I thought it at first, but I would now correct myself as, a moment or two later, I had to correct my first impression. Those cheap little alarm clocks are certainly not ornamental, but they are generally most useful. This one was of a type such as are manufactured in Germany and Switzerland and sold here in England by the thousand at the cost of a few shillings each, principally for use in servants' bedrooms. The watch on my wrist had been a persistent rebel for the past three weeks, and I was at first glad of the presence of this unsightly instrument for the measurement of time. And then I noticed that it was as silent as my own watch, and, although I knew the present time to be seven or thereabouts, the two hands mutely insisted that it was one minute after nine.

I walked across, picked it up, and began to wind it. The mechanism responded with a noise like that of a check winch on a fishing-rod.

'Got the exact time?' I asked Hebden. 'I think I've got some sand in my watch, so I may as well get this chap going.'

He turned abruptly.

'Oh, you're not trying to get that thing going?' he asked. 'You'll be lucky if you do.' He came over and stood behind me. it hasn't gone for these six years and more, and there isn't a clock-repairer who's been able to make it go, although a round dozen have tried their hands.'

'You seem to have taken some trouble over it,' I remarked, wondering why he had taken such pains over three or four shillings worth of mass production. 'What's the matter with it?'

He laughed shortly.

'Well, none of the experts know, but I think I have an inkling. It simply won't go, and that's that. I just had it looked at to see if anyone could advance a scientific reason why it had stopped and couldn't be restarted, and none could. Perhaps you're lucky in a way. Like nearly all these cheap clocks it had a terrible tick, and you'd have thrown it out of the window or at least banished it to the landing. But I keep it because there's a story behind it. It used to belong to Martin Hornbin.'

I was interested at once. Most of us have a morbid streak in us. Hence the money taken at the entrance to the Chamber of Horrors at any waxworks show.

'Of course!' I murmured, 'I was forgetting that you were mixed up in that affair.'
He laughed good-humouredly.

'Mixed up in that affair! I like that. Considering that I didn't appear on the scene until nearly a year later. Yet I suppose in a way I was. It's just possible that I threw the last ounce into the scale which decided a man's fate, and thereby caused a sort of nine days' wonder. I don't often tell the story, because if a man calls me a liar my first instinct is to punch his head, and I don't want life to become one continuous scrap.'

'I won't call you a liar,' I said.

'Thanks!' He laughed and looked down on me. 'Well, even if you did, you wouldn't be big enough to hit. And, besides, you're my guest. Well, if you really want the story I don't mind breaking a rule in your favour. You'll think I've got Ananias beaten still and cold, but there's Dr Brewin to support me, if you care to trouble to write and ask him. And there's still the old clock here. There's an hour to spare before dinner. You'll find me downstairs when you're ready, and I'll tell you all about it over a pipe in the garden.'

I was downstairs at the end of five minutes, when I found him waiting for me, and we walked out into the patches of late sunlight and the long shadows of the scented garden. There was a little preamble while we lit our pipes, and he pointed out to me certain examples of his skill as a horticulturist; then, while we paced the long middle lawn, he told me the story which I am about to re-tell. I cannot, of course, be completely accurate, but I shall use his own words to the best of my recollection.

You know (he said) what happened to me after the war? I'd been one of those fellows who left school in July, 1914, and found themselves in khaki by the middle of August. When peace came along I was nearly twenty-three, with no profession except soldiering, so I stuck in the Service as long as possible. Then, after a year or two, the popular passion for economy got me stuck on the Reserve of Officers and decanted me on a hard, cold world with two or three hundred pounds and no prospects for the future. That was before I came into Aunt's Elinor's legacy, and, although I'd got a microscopical income of my own, I had to learn to do something in order to spread butter on my bread.

Those were the days when every ex-soldier wanted a life in the open air. No stuffy offices, no long hours of routine, but something healthy and strenuous, so that a man could go on feeling that he was a man. Lord knows how many gratuities went west in miserable little poultry farms, run by fellows who knew no more about chickens and eggs than that there was some sort of intimate relation between the two. Poultry tanning had been a bit blown on by the time I left the Army, or I might have gone in for it; but I did the next worst, and got myself taken on as a pupil at fruit-growing and French gardening.

The man who took me on was an old R.E. Colonel. Sappers can do anything except pass a searching test of sanity, and what old Felmer didn't-know about his job you could find room for in the stop-press column of a newspaper on Saturday night. He had acres and acres, all beautifully kept, and grew wonderful stuff; but even then I don't think it would have paid without us pupils.

There were half a dozen of us pupils, and none of us lived with old Felmer. We had to find lodgings for ourselves, and be 'on parade' at godless hours in the morning. We worked pretty well all the time it was light, with the very shortest breaks for meals and so forth. All the other pupils were ex-officers, and we formed a little community of our own and had practically nothing to do with the rest of the village.

I don't mean that we were stand-offish or ungregarious, but we hadn't much time for associating with other people. By the time we'd knocked off for the day we generally wanted to fall straight into bed and lose consciousness. Sometimes we raided the village pub, but nobody beside ourselves seemed to come into the stuffy little parlour at the back, where beer was a penny a pint dearer than in the tap-room. I'm giving you these details to show how it was that I didn't hear much village gossip or local scandal.

You know already that I got digs at Hornbin's farm. I knew, of course, that there was a certain amount of talk going on about him. He was a tall, lean, leathery, grey-whiskered old sinner of fifty or more, and the second Mrs Hornbin was quite a girl, with a sullen sort of rustic prettiness. She'd been his wife for six months, although the first Mrs Hornbin had been dead scarcely a year. In that part of the country they love funerals and wreaths and deep mourning, and they were just the sort of people to resent a second marriage in indecent haste—as they would call it. So although I knew the Hornbins were unpopular I put it down to the old man's aversion to celibacy and the young woman's readiness to meet him half way. But they made me pretty comfortable, and the rest was no business of mine.

Well, now I can start telling you about that clock. I found it in my bedroom on the night of my arrival, and wondered how I was going to endure having it in the room. Like most of those cheap tin clocks it had a very brisk and appallingly loud tick. It was like having a woodpecker in the room. However, it didn't trouble me as much as I expected, for on most subsequent nights I was so dog-tired that I could have slept with a thousand similar clocks all around me. I was always promising myself that I'd buy another, but I had little time and few opportunities, and when I had time and opportunity I somehow always forgot.

Like all clocks with a loud, quick tick, it used to 'talk'. After the alarum had gone off in the morning it used to say: 'Get-up, get-up, get-up, get-up,' until I was irritated into getting out of bed and busying myself with dressing, so that I needn't hear it. It used to talk in a dreary and never-ending iambic rhythm, by which I mean to say that the accentuation always seemed to come on the second beat. On Sunday, when I wasn't compelled to rise early, I used to lie in bed and hear it tell me so. 'It's-Sunday, it's-Sunday, it's-Sunday,' it used to say.

After a bit I found that by exercising my will and imagination I could make the clock seem to say any short sentence over and over again, provided, of course, that the words were suited to the clock's rhythm; and when I had once idly pretended that the clock was actually saying the word, or words, that I wanted it to say it was strange how human the voice began to sound. But until I started teaching it to say things—and I can't describe myself any better— the clock, like a badly trained parrot, seemed to know only two sentences. ' You're-awake, you're-awake, you're-awake,' it used to say before I went to sleep or when I woke in the night, and in the morning there was that irritating 'Get-up, get-up, get-up.' However, after a while, when sometimes I lay idly imagining that it was repeating to me a phrase of my own invention, I noticed subtle changes in it at times. I don't know much about clocks, but I imagine that, especially with the cheap variety, their action is apt to hasten or slow. At any rate, I would sometimes hear a loud click from its interior and then the rhythm would change, so that the words I imagined I was hearing changed too, and there was nothing but a garbled balderdash until I invented some short sentence suitable to the altered beats of time. I dare say you'll think this was a witless sort of amusement and a sign of incipient lunacy, but shut any tired man up in a room with a clock like that breaking in upon his thoughts, and I think, if he were honest, he'd have the same sort of confession to make.

Anyhow, I'm telling you the facts and you can think what you like. If you think that I was on the way to going off my head, there was a time when I should have been disposed to agree with you, as you shall hear. But as yet you haven't begun to hear why.

I came home dead tired as usual on a certain evening, had my supper, nodded and drowsed over the local evening paper, and blundered upstairs to bed. The old 'grandfather' in the parlour said that it was half past nine, but the clock in my room had run down and stopped two or three hours since, and I altered the hands, wound it up, and set the alarm for the morning. And while I was doing this I received the most extraordinary impression.

Briefly, I felt that the clock wanted to talk to me, that it had some message to convey. When the postman has called I don't know if you have ever picked up a letter lying face downwards, and, although the envelope was unfamiliar, known instinctively that it was for you and contained news of great interest or importance? I have. And on those occasions I have been conscious of what people call Personality. Well, that's how I felt about that clock.

I don't mean that the clock itself seemed to have personality or anything analogous to personality, but just as I had picked up letters and known instinctively that here were connecting links between some strong personality and my own, so did I feel about that clock. It had suddenly become a connecting link between some other entity and me. It was a means of communication as ink and paper are means of communication, and I will swear that in touching it I was conscious of an influence which was baleful and sinister and unhappy.

The impression couldn't have lasted more than a second, for I had a dread of becoming morbid, and while I undressed I declined to listen to the loud clattering of the clock. But once in bed, and composing myself for sleep, I had to listen, and, as usual, the clock began 'talking'. And tonight it said something which it had never said before. It said, 'Kate-speaking, Kate-speaking, Kate-speaking,' the same words over and over and over. The thing irritated me at first, and then almost set me laughing when I wondered how my subconscious mind could have invented such rubbish. I didn't, as far as I was aware, know anybody named Kate.

I tried presently to imagine that the clock was saying something else, and this time I failed. It persisted in this one idiotic series of repetitions, and at last I had to bury my head under the clothes to shut out the sound.

It may have been this uncomfortable and unhealthy way of getting sleep which caused me to wake in the middle of the night. The clock seemed to be ticking a little slower, and now it seemed to say very distinctly: 'I-died-here, I-died-here, I-died-here.'

Now mine was the best bedroom in the house, and I had always had a kind of idea that the first Mrs Hornbin had died in it. The thought had never worried me because I hadn't known the lady, I didn't believe in haunted rooms, and anyhow hundreds of people must have died in every bedroom in a very old house. But I must admit that I went hot and cold all over. Of course, I wouldn't admit for a moment to myself that what I heard could be anything but the clock ticking out words which my own imagination had, so to speak, put into its mouth. But I didn't like my sub-consciousness playing me that kind of trick. Eventually I got to sleep somehow and woke in the morning feeling jaded and tired.

On the following night the clock was on its best behaviour when I entered my room. 'You're-awake, you're-awake, you're-awake,' it seemed to say to me as I lay in bed, listening. I hadn't to listen very long either, for falling asleep was as easy that night as coasting down a hill on a bicycle. I don't know what woke me between one and two, but wake I did, and with a very disagreeable sensation. A voice which sounded as human as my own was talking in the room, and it was saying only one word and a very unpleasant word at that. As dreary and monotonous as the note of a single chapel bell, but with a droning sadness impossible to describe, the Voice was saying, 'Mur-dered, mur-dered, mur-dered.'

In an instant I was sweating all over, and although I seemed to wake to full consciousness, I swear that it took me an appreciable time to realise that I was listening to no human voice but merely the ticking of the clock. It kept slowly ticking out that one word, and if you want to know what a beastly word it really is, just shut yourself up in the dark and repeat it to yourself slowly for a few times.

I sat up in bed there, staring at the clock, and went on sweating. It may seem very absurd to you, but I daren't even get up and put the clock outside. I was afraid to touch the thing.

I don't know how long I endured the Chinese torture of having that word drilled into my head. It must have been half an hour at least. At the end of that time, when I was expecting every moment to go raving mad, something in the thing's innards gave a click, and the ticks came quicker. It gave up droning out 'Mur-dered', but the new word it seemed to have learned wasn't much better. 'Ar-se-nic, ar-sen-ic, ar-sen-ic,' was the new word.

Well, I don't know how I got to sleep that night, but somehow I managed to lose consciousness, and woke in the morning—when the alarm went off—feeling pretty cheap. To be frank, I was in a dead funk. It didn't occur to me seriously that the clock might be a means by which Somebody or Something was able to communicate with me. I thought, naturally enough, that my mind was going. And yet, 'Kate speaking—I died here—murdered—arsenic'—well, it did make some kind of sense, didn't it?

The thought that I was going batty haunted me all day, so when I knocked off work that night I went straight and saw Dr Brewin, whom I hadn't met before. He was quite a young chap with an unprofessional manner when dealing with men of his own sort and age.

'Well,' he said, 'and what do you think is the matter with you?'

'I think,' I answered, 'that I'm going mad.'

'Literally?'

'Literally.'

He laughed good-humouredly and reassuringly.

'Well, that's a good symptom,' he said. 'Most people who are going that way haven't the least idea of it. Sit down and tell me all about it.'

I did. I told him what I've just told you. He gave me a smile which was somehow sly and yet penetrating.

'Ah!' he said. 'Who's been listening to local scandal?'

'I haven't—if you mean that for me,' I said.

'Oh! But I thought you lodged with the Hornbins!'

'So I do, but they'd hardly talk scandal about themselves. I suppose you think that because I knew the old man had married again so soon after his first wife's death'

'My dear sir,' he interrupted me, 'do you mean to tell me that you've been here for months and not heard anything said about old Hornbin?'

I told him I hadn't; and why. Still he seemed not inclined to believe me.

'I'm going to trust you not to let this go any further,' he said presently, 'I wasn't here when the first Mrs Hornbin died. Old Wake had the practice, and he was treating Mrs Hornbin for some gastric trouble. He was a dying man himself at the time, and perhaps didn't trouble much when Mrs Hornbin died suddenly. He signed the certificate without making an examination. From what I can hear the symptoms were not incompatible with arsenic poisoning, and local opinion is to the effect that Mrs Hornbin would have got better if he hadn't helped her into the next world.'

He paused and we stared at each other.

'I'm a doctor,' he continued, 'I don't profess to know anything about spirits. I don't believe in them and I don't disbelieve. But suppose there were such things and one of them wanted to send a message—as poor Mrs Hornbin might be supposed to want to send one—I don't see why she shouldn't use that clock if she couldn't speak for herself.'

It was a ghastly thought, but it was comforting to know that he saw no signs of lunacy in me.

'What's to be done?' I asked.

'I don't know. I've had half a mind to look into the matter a long time ago. Local gossip, you know. It won't have been the first time that local gossip's been the cause of an exhumation. But I've done nothing yet, because I really haven't had sufficient cause to meddle. But now—well, I think I shall go and see the Chief Constable. You've just about turned the scale.'

'And what'll happen?' I asked, with a funny tight feeling in my throat.

'Oh, if he thinks as I do there'll be a post-mortem. It'll all be done quietly and privately. Another little job for Dr Bee.'

He meant, of course, the great pathologist whose name was, and still is, a household word. I went home comforted, but more mystified than ever, and I couldn't help shrinking from the sight of old Hornbin in the kitchen. After what I'd heard the man began to look to me like a murderer.

When I got to my room that night, what do you think that infernal clock was saying? It was ticking away triumphantly and saying:

'They've got him! They've got him! They've got him!'

I put it out on the landing and risked not waking in time. And in doing so I almost dropped it, because I couldn't bear the feel of the thing.

Well, you know most of the rest. They came and arrested Hornbin about a fortnight later. The woman was found to have died of arsenic poisoning, and suspicion, followed by proof, settled on her husband.

Of course, I had to leave the farm then, but I took the clock with me as a souvenir.

They hanged Hornbin at Wandsworth at nine o'clock one morning. You can see for yourself what time the clock stopped. It hasn't gone again from that day to this.

For The Local Rag

Early in December it was customary for Mr Marvell, the editor and proprietor of the Foxbridge Independent, to edge his way into the reporters'-room and say to Dorby:

'Oh, Dorby, about our Christmas supplement. Weil have a short story from you as usual this year. Have it ready in plenty of time, won't you?'

And Dorby would say: 'Yes, sir, thank you. The usual sort of short story?'

'Yes; something—h'm—sentimental, you know. Holly and mistletoe, and families being reunited and—h'm—enemies forgiving each other on Christmas Eve.'

And Dorby would go home and write something which he fondly believed Charles Dickens would have approved, full of the Christmas spirit, with aged and starving parents being surprised on the eve of Noel by the return of a prodigal son or daughter burdened with hitherto unsuspected wealth and laden with presents. For this he received thirty shillings—which relived Mr Marvell from the embarrassment of feeling that he ought to have made his faithful employee a little present.

The total population of Foxbridge did not exceed eleven thousand, and the circulation of the Independent was proportionally small. Like more ambitious newspapers, it relied largely on advertisements for its revenue. Mr Marvell had no difficulty in getting sufficient of these to make a comfortable little income. Auctioneers' notices, servants wanted, agricultural implements, manures and land dressings, bargain weeks at the local shops, all were grist that came to that dusty little mill set in an alley behind the High Street. And, as Dorby could tell you, Mr Marvell kept the expenses of the paper very low. But at Christmas-time Mr Marvell lashed out. He published a supplement as a kind of Christmas box to his readers. You could rely on finding some syndicated articles on Old Christmas Customs, Christmas Games, a revolting Household Hint or two on what to do with a stale turkey or how to make mincemeat go twice as far, and always a short story by Charles Dorby—with the title in huge Old English letters intertwined with holly and mistletoe.

Charles Dorby was the chief reporter. As a matter of fact, he was the only reporter, for you could hardly count Monkland, the pimply boy of sixteen who seemed to come to no harm through wearing canvas shoes all the year round. So far Monkland could only be trusted to report cricket and football matches. He had not yet learned to read his own shorthand, and he had a fascinating gift of misreporting speeches and, in the fresh innocence of his youth, making 'floaters' which, if undetected at the office, might have involved Mr Marvell in heavy legal expenses. The bulk of the labour therefore fell on Dorby's shoulders, and he was thus overworked besides being underpaid.

Dorby was a little man of indeterminate age, and he wore the dejected air of a dog which had been chained up too long. He was secretly proud of his calling, but used long since to being snubbed, patronised, and abused. He was proud of the Independent and simmered under the surface in mild rages when he heard it described as 'the local rag'. True, it wasn't run quite as he would have run it if he had had full control. It wasn't quite so independent as it sounded. He knew quite well that Mr Marvell increased his modest revenue by accepting presents for leaving something out or putting something else in. And the world's worst poetess since Eliza Cook enclosed a postal order for ten shillings with each of her effusions.

Dorby, then, was a small man of dejected aspect, and this was accentuated by a drooping moustache, which Mrs Dorby in her maiden state had thought silky and fascinating. He had married in his intrepid youth, when he still dreamed of coming to London and editing The Times, a local music-teacher, who was responsible for most of the desolating noises which the young bourgeoisie of Foxbridge knocked out of their untuned cottage pianos. The Dorbys were not more unhappy than the average married couple with a family and a very slender income. There were two boys who relieved Dorby of some embarrassment by winning scholarships to the local Grammar School. He wanted them to become journalists!

In his spare time—yes, he managed to find a little spare time—Dorby wrote short stories, and occasionally these were accepted by obscure publications. Dorby's chances came when the editor of a would-be popular weekly found himself short on the day of going to press. He was a really terrible writer of the worst kind of journalese, and all the most worn cliches were as dear to him as his wife and family. If your eye happened first to catch the substantive you could guess the adjective. A barrister? Well, of course, he was 'rising' and 'young'. A chasm? Naturally it was 'yawning'. A void? Not very surprisingly it was an empty void. And his characters all talked as if they were living in the eighteen-eighties—and proud of it, too! But Dorby knew not of his own treasonable assaults on the King's English. In his own funny little way he was inordinately vain. If a friend met him at Christmas-time in the local Constitutional Club, and said, 'Oh, Dorby, old man, that was a jolly good yam of yours in the supplement of the local rag,' he felt like a schoolboy who had just won the mile open, and forgot the offensive name by which his paper had been called.

I have been generalising, of course, meaning all the while to come to a certain day in Dorby's life. The boy Monkland, obviously, was not always sixteen. He had been younger, and he will unfortunately grow older unless his canvas shoes lead him to the grave by way of pleurisy and pneumonia. I do not know the exact date of the day I have in mind; I only know that it was early in December and that it was snowing. The time was early afternoon, but it was already dusk, for the clouds which were shedding the snow had shut out the failing sunlight. Dorby sat on a high stool in the reporters'-room, transcribing shorthand notes into longhand with the grudging assistance of a blue flicker of a gaslight overhead.

He had been to a wedding, and he hated weddings; still he had to go. The boy Monkland had once been entrusted with a wedding, and, quite innocently, had written in his report something so shocking that, but for the sharp-eyed compositor, the subsequent and inevitable legal proceedings must have ruined Mr Marvell. This had been a bad wedding, even as weddings went. The bride's people, a frugal family, had, it seemed, detailed a relative to steer the reporter away from the refreshment buffet. Dorby preferred funerals. At funerals the bereaved were generally so distressed as not to care what became of the ham sandwiches.

Dorby went through his notes. Had he a full list of presents? Yes, he had. Heavens, how many fish-slices had been bestowed on that happy couple? It looked like the shopping-list of a monastery in Lent. Could he call it 'A Fashionable Foxbridge Wedding'? If he did the county people wouldn't like it, and if he didn't the townsfolk would be offended. Well, one can't please everybody in this complicated world.

Still, there was snow falling and Christmas was coming on. Dorby loved the merry Yuletide— as he invariably described it. When he had dealt faithfully by this hateful wedding, he knew that he would feel quite Christmassy and sentimental. It was about time that Mr Marvell came in and reminded him about the Christmas story.

And it was at that very moment that Mr Marvell actually came in, with the promptness of a familiar spirit responding to an incantation.

'Oh, Dorby,' he said, 'leave out that report about the affiliation case. The man's people have been to see me and—h'm—you know—I don't think any good purpose would be served by publishing it. You can fill up the space by writing something about the real Father Christmas who will be at Judson's Toy Bazaar. They've sent us a quarter-page ad., and it won't hurt to write them up a bit.'

Mr Marvell edged himself a little further into the room. He could not get in very far, because the room was merely a cubby-hole. There was no available space for Dorby to entertain callers. He could not spread his arms beyond the margins of the narrow desk without soiling his elbows with the dust from old files of the paper which had been kept for some unknown, but probably morbid, reason.

'And,' Mr Marvell continued, 'you'd like to do a story for the supplement as usual, I s'pose?'

Dorby looked up.

'Yes, sir. Thank you. Same sort as usual?'

Mr Marvell screwed up his liberally whiskered countenance and rolled his eyes in an effort to concentrate his thoughts. He might have been a publisher trying to make up his mind if it would be worthwhile to bring out an edition de luxe of the works of some precious but not too popular author.

'No,' he said slowly, 'I think not.'

Dorby had written the story for the supplement on each occasion for the past twenty years, and year by year Mr Marvell had been growing more and more conscious of an element of 'sameness' about them. Prodigal sons had returned home on Christmas Eve with a punctuality highly creditable to the railway systems, which were generally disorganised at that time of year. Old enemies had shaken hands or embraced according to whether they belonged to the same sex or not. Peace children had brought the Christmas Spirit into sordid homes. Church bells had pealed out their messages of peace and good will. Modest maidens had surrendered—verbally, at least—to dashing young men while the carols were being sung. On the whole Mr Marvell was conservative, but he believed in a change now and again.

'I tell you what,' he said. 'Write us a ghost story.'

'A what?' said Dorby. Dorby's face did not fall, because it had fallen years ago and had, so to say, stayed down; nor did his tone indicate the dismay in which the request had suddenly plunged him. It merely suggested that he thought he might not have heard aright. Mr Marvell might have said goats instead of ghosts. 'A what?' he asked again.

Mr Marvell responded quite airily.

'Ghost story,' he repeated. 'Christmas ghost story. You know, old country houses—panelled walls—spectre with clanking chains—missing will, or hidden treasure. You know the sort of thing.'

'Yes, sir,' said Dorby. 'Very well.'

If Mr Marvell had told Dorby to write a tragedy in blank verse after one of the Elizabethan models, Dorby would have said, 'Very well!' and gone home and had a shot at it; and he would have owned himself to be no journalist had he failed to produce something. Mr Marvell, quite unaware of the shattering effects of his order, then nodded and withdrew. You must know Dorby a little better to understand why the blow that had fallen on him was indeed a blow.

First of all Dorby was proud of his old-fashioned Christmas stories. He secretly regarded himself as a second Dickens, but deprived of general recognition by the stupidity of the public and a general conspiracy on the part of most editors and publishers. He had looked forward to writing that Christmas story for the supplement and afterwards receiving the congratulations of a few sentimental old women and one or two insincere male friends. It was his star turn, and now he had been robbed of doing it by a mere editorial caprice.

In the second place, Dorby did not believe in ghosts. He believed in a great many things which leave most men sceptical, but not in ghosts. He was well-known in the town and had made no secret of his views. For so mild a man he had said some quite cruel things about superstitions and the superstitious, and said them publicly. Now there would be a great deal of ribald laughter in the town when it became known that old Dorby had written a ghost story.

Ghosts! How could such things exist? When you died you went to Heaven if you had been good, or to Hell if you had been wicked or bad, or perhaps only just ordinary. How could anybody come back? If you were in Heaven you wouldn't want to, and if you were in the other place you jolly well couldn't! This was logic. Only the subscribers to an almost unmentionable creed, and a few loose-thinking people with practically no religion at all, believed in a middle state in which souls were neither yet at peace nor eternally condemned.

Again, he did not know how to write a ghost story. He hated such things and had never read one except on rare occasions when he had been led astray by the dishonest methods employed by the author. Yet what was he to do? Refuse the commission and lose the thirty shillings? That was quite unthinkable. Besides, to do so would be a tacit confession of his failure as a journalist. A journalist, he held, should be able to write something about anything on the shortest notice.

It was then, while he continued knocking his 'wedding' copy into shape, that he renewed his regrets for having quarrelled with Rennick.

Rennick was the only man in the town in Dorby's station of life whom he felt that he was meeting on terms of intellectual equality. The interests of the local tradesmen were few and material, and instead of looking up to Charles Dorby as a representative of the Fourth Estate they were apt to pity him for being an over-driven and underpaid hack. Rennick, though, was different. Rennick was a little dried-up man of fifty, clerk to the principal lawyer in the town. He, too, was poor, for although he knew most of the villainies perpetrated by his employer during the past thirty years, he lacked the blackmailing touch, and his salary remained disgracefully small. But he was not fond of money. His tastes marched a long way with those of Dorby. He knew his Dickens and his Trollope, and spoke highly of a certain Henry James, whose works Dorby often tried hard to enjoy, but who invariably defeated him and sent him to bed with a headache.

Also Rennick was a mine of odd scraps of local information and forgotten folklore. He knew how many horses had been stabled by Oliver Cromwell in the parish church, and the site of a battle which had taken place outside the town during the Wars of the Roses, and where the Duke of Y and Lord X had fought a duel during the eighteenth century, and the spot where the last of the fairies was supposed to have been seen by a plumber late on Boxing Night. Rennick was just the man to know of some ghostly legend which could be twisted into a tale. In that case there would be the added attraction of local colour. But three months ago he had quarrelled with old Rennick, and they were not now on speaking terms.

It has been said that only a fighting man should keep a fighting dog, because a dog of that nature is sure to lead his master into trouble sooner or later. Neither Dorby nor Rennick could have been described as fighting men, but their respective dogs were about as pacific as two adjacent Balkan States.

Rennick owned an Irish-terrier which was a sort of canine Tybalt and regarded every other dog as a Montague. Dorby owned a pugnacious mongrel, with perhaps rather more bull in it than anything else, which he had bought as a pup under the delusion that it was a pure-bred fox-terrier. Of course, neither had the least control over his dog, and the result was inevitable.

The men and the dogs met one Sunday morning, and while the two men were discussing the unemployment problem the two dogs made acquaintance in the unconventional manner of their kind. Then Rennick's dog bristled all over and rumbled like an empty stomach, and Dorby's dog, having made a rude and quite unmistakable gesture of contempt, uttered distant thunder in his throat. Of course, both men shouted 'come here', and, of course, neither dog took the least notice. A moment later events were moving at such a pace that it was impossible to distinguish one dog from the other.

That was perhaps how it was that Rennick came to smite Dorby's dog with his umbrella, and Dorby did violence to Rennick's dog with a rather futile little partridge cane. But why describe the childish scene that followed? Each man took his own dog's part, and each blamed the other for not keeping his dog under control. They quarrelled like a pair of flustered old hens giving each other little verbal pecks. They parted in anger, having said just enough to hurt each other. When they met again Dorby tried to look down at the drooping ends of his own moustache and Rennick looked pointedly in another direction. They had not spoken since.

Tomorrow was press day, and besides being chief reporter Dorby was also chief sub-editor and had to get everything ready for 'putting the paper to bed'. He finished his notes about the wedding, and wrote a few lines about Judson's Toy Bazaar and his Father Christmas, to take the place of a police court case which Mr Marvell, on receipt of five pounds, had considered too unsavoury to be reported in detail. Where was Monkland's football copy? Oh, there it was. 'County Senior Cup—Foxbridge's Slashing Victory'. Same old stuff. Monkland was a partisan and had once been charged with the impropriety of booing the referee from the Press box. Foxbridge were always gaining slashing victories or suffering narrow defeats. Mustn't forget to leave room for a report of the Wesleyan Mission Tea Social which would come in this evening, and the Bowling Club annual dinner which would come in tomorrow morning. Thank Heaven the Wesleyans and the Bowling Club did their own reporting. It was quite slack for the day before press day. He could go home quite early.

Yes, and then he'd have to tackle that beastly ghost story!

All the while he had been attending to the needs of the paper his mind had been elsewhere. The quarrel with Rennick and the prospect of having to write a ghost story were as two weights dragging at him. The one affected the other. If he hadn't quarrelled with Rennick he could have gone round to his house that evening and said: 'Rennick, old man, give us an idea with a bit of local colour in it. I've got to write a rotten ghost story this year, instead of one of the good old-fashioned Christmassy sort.'

And then a happy thought struck him. If he couldn't write a sentimental Christmas story this year, at least he could live one. It had never before occurred to him to forgive Rennick. After all, the quarrel was very foolish and trifling. Why shouldn't he go round to Rennick and say: 'Rennick, old man, it's getting on for Christmas, the season of peace and goodwill. I'll own I was in the wrong'—although he didn't really believe that—'let's shake hands and be friends again?'

He knew that Rennick would respond, just as he himself would have responded if Rennick had made the first advance. Each had been looking for a sign from the other. It would be all very pleasant and very Christmassy, and would more then compensate him for the pleasant little task of which he had been deprived. After all, it is far better to experience something delightful than merely to write about it. Then he and Rennick would go off arm-in-arm to the Constitutional Club and take something to moisten the new cement of their friendship. Or perhaps Rennick would have 'something' in the house—which would be even better.

Dashed if he wouldn't do it! It was a fine idea. What funny things men were! Here was he, who had written scores of stories about quarrels being made up at Christmas-time, prepared until a minute or two since to nurse a stupid little grudge and greet an old friend with a scowl.

Dorby's heart lightened suddenly. Even the prospect of writing the ghost story was not so dismal and irritating. Certainly he would go and see Rennick. Wait a minute, hadn't he heard that Rennick was laid up, or had been laid up? A cold or a touch of 'flu or something. Well, that only made it the more likely that he would find him at home.

It was quite dark outside when Dorby left the office, and snow was still falling. As he came out in to the High Street the illuminated dial of the clock outside the town hall, shining like a full moon, informed him that it was twenty-eight minutes past four. Snow was beginning to lie on the pavements, but traffic had so far kept the roads clear. Dorby lived in one of a row of villas some half a mile distant on the outskirts of the town. He set off briskly enough, but after a few moments the sight of a grocer's window tempted him to loiter.

A grocer's window, well lit and packed with crackers and dried fruits, looked more Christmassy to Dorby than any other sight in the world. For a moment or two he stood gloating over it. Then a car drew up close against the kerb behind him, and a voice addressed him.

'That you, Dorby? If you're going home I can give you a lift.'

The speaker was young Mr Packham, the auctioneer, and to reach his home he must pass Dorby's. Dorby thanked him gratefully and climbed in beside him. The car went forward.

Two or three hundred yards distant, on the near side of the street, was the shop of Mr Munko, a dealer in second-hand furniture and books. When on foot Dorby always looked in at the window. It would not be safe to guess how many hundreds of times he and Rennick had turned over the contents of the threepenny box in the hope of finding a first edition worth hundreds of pounds. Mr Munko, however, had other views.

The blood of nearly every known tribe of the human race was mingled in the veins of Mr Munko. It would be safe to say that none of his ancestors had married anyone hailing from within a thousand miles of his birthplace. Mr Munko, despite a tendency to scream when he became excited, had a level head. Such men are not fools in business. One never found anything in the threepenny box much more exciting than the sermons of some defunct and forgotten clergyman whose innocence had been exploited by wicked publishers. But he and Rennick had never quite given up hope.

The thought that he was approaching the shop put Dorby once more in mind of Rennick. Then, as the car drew near, Dorby was a little surprised to see Rennick standing bareheaded in the fluttering snowflakes, peering in through the shop windows. Rather silly of him, Dorby thought, to stand about bareheaded in the snow so soon after having had a chill or a touch of 'flu.

Dorby had no doubt but that it was Rennick even before the little man turned and faced the street. The shape of the figure, its poise with bent head and short-sighted stare were unmistakable. An instant later the car was passing, and then Rennick turned, looked straight into Dorby's face, and gave him the friendliest of friendly smiles.

Dorby acted on an impulse.

'Would you mind stopping just for one second?' he said to Packham.

'Eh? Oh, very well. Only do be quick!'

The car stopped. Dorby clambered out and ran back. Rennick was waiting in the ungenerous light which filtered through Mr Munko's dirty windows.

'I say, old man,' Dorby exclaimed breathlessly, 'I want to make it up! Sorry we had that stupid quarrel. May I come round and see you this evening?'

Rennick nodded and gave him again the very friendly smile. He did not speak, but the nod and the smile quite plainly said: 'All right, old man, come round by all means, but we won't talk about it now.' This was all Dorby wanted. Packham, he gathered, was in a hurry. He turned and trotted back to the car.

'Sorry to hurry you,' Packham said. 'Thought you wanted to buy something, not only just go and look in the window. But I promised to be home sharp at half-past four, and it's that now.'

Five minutes later, having shaken the loose snow off his coat, Dorby entered his small dining-room, where Mrs Dorby was hugging an economical fire. She rose immediately and began to prepare his high tea.

Mrs Dorby was a depressed little woman who believed that it was healthy and economical to feed her family on stuff that came out of tins. There was no waste, she would say; and there wasn't, because all scraps were eaten, even after they had been kept a perilous length of time. Still, none of them had yet suffered from ptomaine poisoning, and had Dorby been one of those men who aspire to breaking records he might have claimed to have eaten more tinned salmon than any other living man. It was tinned salmon this evening. While he ate and drank, Dorby shared his new grievance with his life partner. Mrs Dorby was herself, and not without cause, a painstaking and highly efficient grumbler, and Dorby lost few opportunities of letting her know that his life wasn't all honey.

'A ghost story!' he exclaimed, disgust on his face and in his voice. 'Who believes in ghosts nowadays! It's childish. It's against nature and it's against religion. And I could have written something to make people feel that there's still some goodness in human nature. But, no—a ghost story!'

'Need it be about a real ghost, dear?' Mrs Dorby asked, 'I mean to say, I read a pretty little story in a ladies' paper once. It was about a young lady who was put into a haunted room. The room wasn't really haunted, of course, but supposed to be. And in the middle of the night the ghost came in and frightened her. But it wasn't a real ghost, it was a man dressed up in a sheet. So,' Mrs Dorby concluded simply, 'she married him.'

'Pah!' said Dorby.

'Couldn't you write something like that, dear?'

'No, I couldn't. I suppose if Marvell says he wants a ghost story he means a real ghost story. Why couldn't he let me write about something that I believe in? I believe in humanity, I believe in Christmas, I believe in Charles Dickens. But ghosts!'

'You're always saying that a good journalist ought to be able to write about anything,' commented Mrs Dorby.

'Oh, so I could, I suppose,' he answered moodily, 'but it doesn't say I want to. I suppose I shall get hold of some silly local legend and twist something out of it. At six o'clock I'm going to step round to see old Rennick'

'Rennick? But I thought'

'Pooh,' said Dorby, 'that's all over now. I met him in the High Street about half-past four, and he was quite friendly. I don't bear any malice. He knew he was in the wrong and he apologised.'

Dorby believed in maintaining his dignity in the home even at the expense of truth. It was his dignity which had caused him to select six o'clock as the hour of his call. Very soon his boys would be home from school, and the elder, Sidney—yes, I am afraid they called him Sid—was involved in the mysteries of quadratic equations. Dorby, who had lived most of his life under the delusion that algebra was an Oriental language, did not know what a quadratic equation was, but he was not going to expose his ignorance to a younger and critical generation. By six o'clock the boys would have had their tea and would start discussing their homework; and that was the time for Dorby to go.

Events proved that he had timed his departure almost to the minute. At the first glance of a Hall and Knight and an exercise book Dorby rose and prepared to go out.

It was a wretched evening. It had stopped snowing, but the wind had veered east and cut through his thin overcoat like a cold knife. As he walked he huddled himself in his clothes.

What a life it was! An editor who wanted to make him write about something he didn't believe in, a son who wanted to be told about quadratic equations, and now this brutal east wind! Still, he was going to make friends again with old Rennick, and that was something. Dorby estimated that Rennick's home was ten minutes' walking distance from his own, but on this occasion, spurred by the desire to keep warm, he covered the ground in eight.

The house was very dark and silent. Not a light anywhere. Dorby pressed the electric bell three or four times without attracting attention from within, and shivered on the doorstep for four or five minutes before coming to the conclusion that the Rennicks were all out. He was in the act of turning when he heard flat and heavy footfalls approach the door from the other side, and a faint and muffled voice—Mrs Rennick's voice—called out: 'Yes? Who is it?' Dorby answered, and the door was hesitatingly opened. Mrs Rennick stared at him across the threshold. She showed him a face which was very white save for the eyes, and these were red-rimmed and swollen.

Like so many small men, Rennick had taken himself a wife of noble proportions who had grown mountainous in middle age. Dorby had now only to look at her to see that there was something wrong. The long channels running down her flaccid cheeks were now watercourses for tears.

'Mrs Rennick,' he exclaimed. 'What's the matter?'

'Haven't you heard?' she faltered. 'I thought that was perhaps why'

'I haven't heard anything. Tell me.'

'My husband. My dear husband. He took to his bed three weeks ago. He thought it was only a chill. He wouldn't let me send for a doctor. I d-didn't until—until it was too late. It was pneumonia.'

Dorby stared and then reeled forward. A kind of sickness seized him. All that he had believed was shattered and came toppling around him like the ruins of a falling tower. He buried his face in the wet sleeve of his coat and leaned against the doorpost, whimpering. He knew instinctively what he was going to hear. The voice of Mrs Rennick came to him like something heard in a dream:

'He died ... at half past four . . . this afternoon.'

The Boy With Red Hair

After the little comer shop had been broken into, and Henry Gilkes killed by a blow over the head from a jemmy, and a week's takings abstracted from a drawer in the parlour, the intelligentsia of Scotland Yard, which was presently asked to take an interest in the affair, agreed with the county police that it was the work of a beginner.

Most aggravating of all the aggravating circumstances attached to the case was the fact that the assassin had actually been seen, but little Frank Gilkes, who had rushed downstairs after his father on that tragic night, was almost worse than useless to the big, patient man who plagued him hour after hour with question after question.

Poor little Frank Gilkes was only nine years old, and the detectives had need of their patience, for he had an impediment in his speech which his terrible late experiences had not tended to alleviate. He had heard a noise downstairs, his father had rushed down, and he had got up and run down after his father. Grim reconstructions in the very room inevitably followed. His father was lying there, and the other man stood here with an iron bar in his hand. He was a big, tall man with dreadful eyes. No, he c-c-couldn't say how the man was dressed, and he h-h-hadn't seen him before. And that was all they were every able to get from the boy.

The shop stood at a corner of a row of small villas on the outskirts of a small and depressing provincial town. Cigarettes and sweets and groceries were to be bought there, and the word groceries embraced an assortment of articles ranging from bootlaces to slices of cold meat. It was a useful shop for anybody in the immediate neighbourhood who had suddenly run short of something, and the slipshod housekeeping of the local matrons had been the gain of Henry Gilkes. They were for ever popping in—as they termed it—for sugar, or tea, or 'popped in' for sweets, and their husbands for Woodbines and Players. The shop was seldom empty, although only the more discerning realised the comparative magnitude of Henry Gilkes's apparently modest business.

Gilkes was in the habit of banking on Thursday mornings, and the robbery and murder had taken place on a Wednesday night, when more money was likely to be found on the premises than at any other time. It took, therefore, no great effort of deduction to assume that the wanted man knew Gilkes and his habits. For the rest, the crime was stamped all over with the hallmark of the amateur. But the big man with the dreadful eyes was never found, and the hounds of the law bayed on false scent after false scent, and slowly relinquished the chase. Within a year the murderer had an undisputed place in the shadowy gallery of undiscovered criminals.

Ernest Peckham was not a big man, although he looked big to a boy of nine. Nor were his eyes dreadful, except at that time when he first wore the stigmata of Cain. Normally they were deep blue eyes, merry and kindly and utterly deceptive, and they went well with a round, chubby, rosy face. Fie was not more than five feet four in height, generous when he had the means, fond of animals, attractive to women, and generally popular in his restricted circle. As is quite common in such cases, he was the last man who could be suspected of such a crime; and it was a fact that nobody ever did suspect him.

The man was then twenty-nine, and he called himself a canvasser. He lived at Calby Cross, five miles distant from the site of the Weybury murder. He spent his days touting in the mean streets of half a dozen towns and villages, trying with varying success to induce working-class women to buy cheap finery, drapery, blankets, and flashy jewellery on the instalment system. He was good at his work, having an attractive smile, and a flair for telling the kind of joke which was best appreciated. When instalments lapsed he was no more harsh than the firm of Levy & Garstein compelled him to be. Everybody liked young Ernie Peckham.

It is not altogether a good thing for a man earning two pounds ten a week to taste the sweets of popularity. Such compliments as he received he must return in the same liquid measure. Moreover, there were horses which, much more often than not, belied the written word of the newspaper prophet, and football teams whose sudden lapses of form perpetually defeated his purpose of naming four home and one away.

So it happened that early one January he shared with the firm of Levy & Garstein a difficulty in balancing his accounts, and another was sent in his place to tempt the working-class wives and daughters to part from their shillings. He found himself a cipher in the published returns of the unemployed, and spent a long month practically without beer and tobacco, while he got deeper and deeper into debt with his landlady.

He had no thought at first of visiting that shop at the corner of Gaylard Road, Weybury, or of doing anything else which might put him on the wrong side of the law. He had never imagined himself to be anything but honest. But as one long and dreary day followed another, an incident which lingered in his memory burned deeper and deeper into his consciousness.

On a certain Thursday morning, not many weeks since, he had gone from door to door through the meaner streets of Weybury, and, finding himself short of cigarettes, he had entered the little general shop at the corner of Gaylard Road. He had to wait his turn to be served, for the shop was crowded. Above the babble of gossiping women he heard a voice at the counter, and saw a messenger from the public-house across the road holding out a five-pound note. 'Please, Mr Gilkes, could you change this?'

Mr Gilkes, filling a narrow valley between two mountains of tins on the counter, shook his head.

'Sorry, you're unlucky,' he said genially. 'I've just banked right up. Thursdays is my day. Come an hour ago and I could have done it—or a hundred if you'd liked. Wait a moment, though. I've taken some since, and I'll just look to make sure.'

He hurried through an open doorway into the room behind the shop.

Taking no particular interest in the proceedings, Peckham heard the unlocking of a flimsy drawer. Then the shopman returned.

'Sorry,' he said. 'Can't do more than two-ten. Send the rest over later, if you like. Now if you'd come yesterday, or earlier'

And now, weeks later, Ernest Peckham began to think seriously about that little shop. It was so easy! And a Wednesday night was obviously the time. Change a hundred on a Wednesday, could he? Lucky man. Still, for a long time Peckham did no more than think, and went about looking in vain for another job.

Queenie Smith, who worked at the laundry, was the innocent cause of his making up his mind. He was fairly confident that she loved him, but there were four or five other fellows after her, and in these days you never knew quite where you were with a girl. And it wasn't to be expected that a girl was going to wait for ever for a bloke who was out of work. Meanwhile, there was Gilkes's shop—always Gilkes's shop—and it was so easy.

Quite a number of ugly crimes have been committed by men normally and conventionally in love with decent women. Only the Recording Angel knows how many undetected thieves and murderers have subsequently become model husbands. Ernest Peckham had no thought of killing, and the crowbar which he took with him was intended merely for the common purposes of burglary. He rode over on a bicycle that Wednesday night, and hid it in a field close to Gaylard Road.

Ten thousand times during the following weeks he assured himself that he hadn't meant to kill Gilkes. He had just lost his head and struck out. The fool shouldn't have interfered just as he was preparing to go.

It was all like a nightmare to remember, vague and terrible and shadowy—that which had happened in the little room, his dashing back into the road, and his mad ride through loneliness and darkness, with Gaylard Road waking behind him in a tumult of screams and shouts and the blowing of police whistles. The police never found out about the bicycle. He was safe back at Calby Cross while they still hunted the town and the adjacent fields.

Only one incident remained distinct in the man's memory, and one face looked out clearly through the hellish mists of nightmare. It was not the dead man's face. Never afterwards was he to close his eyes without seeing a little boy in a flannel nightshirt, who appeared in a doorway, mouthing and stammering—a little boy with red hair and a chalk-white face.

Fear multiplied the man's brutality, 'I ought to have done the kid in, too! He'll be my death for this!' Afterwards he could never understand why he had spared the boy, or why he had killed the father, for no frightened man understands his secret springs of action. There remained the ghastly fact that he had left behind a witness who might someday weave a rope for his neck.

The boy's red hair and his impediment of speech added a thousand-fold to the terror which chance had lent to his pathetic personality. He stood beside the door, staring through dilated eyes, and trying to say something.

'You—you—you,' and, 'Oh—oh—oh,' and then, 'What—what—what.' A meaningless stuttering and gasping, grief and horror and fear all trying at once to find expression—no more than that. But he heard the words persistently as one hears voices in delirium, and to the end of his days he was haunted not by the man whom he had killed, but by the boy whom he had spared.

He was scarcely reassured when he read in the papers the boy's description of him. 'That kid'll be my death,' he told himself hopelessly time and again. But he was not a big man, as the child had described him, and his eyes, although the glass showed him their anxiety, were not dreadful.

The takings of the robbery amounted to some few shillings short of a hundred and twenty-six pounds, nearly all of which was in Treasury notes. The notes were nearly all old ones, culled from here, there, and everywhere, and he was confident that they were untraceable. Except for the boy he would have felt perfectly safe.

Ernest Peckham developed caution and found himself possessed of an unsuspected fund of low' cunning. He conquered the instinct which bade him vanish from the neighbourhood, realising that this would be the surest way to attract suspicion, and he was very careful to continue to appear penniless. He continued to cadge for drinks and fags in his favourite public-houses.

He grew more confident as time went on, and recovered still more of his nerve; but the sight of a policeman always chilled him, and he could not endure seeing red hair or hearing a person stammer. Also he picked up an odd job or two, and this gave him an excuse for breaking in a little on his secret hoard of money.

A few weeks later the Lincolnshire Handicap was run, and, prior to the race, the newspapers published the fact that a North-country bookmaker had backed his own discredited horse to win him a fortune. Ernest Peckham put a shilling each way on the horse with two different street bookmakers, and told everybody that he had backed it. When White Bud had won at sixty-six to one he had every excuse for appearing in funds. After all, one has not to plunge very desperately on a sixty-six-to-one-chance to win a hundred pounds or so. Fortune, at that time, and for a long while later, seemed persistently to favour the evildoer.

Now that he was able to make use of his money openly, Peckham set himself up in business as a tallyman. He knew the tricks of the trade, and he had a ready-made clientele. He became a thorn in the sensitive flesh of Messrs Levy and Garstein. He bought a second-hand Ford car in order to cover more ground, and a year later he married Queenie Smith. He was safe now—safe except for the red-haired boy who stammered.

The boy continued to haunt Peckham. He was not a superstitious man, but he lived in the shadow of his own doom, and endured all the agonies of a thousand different anticipations. Sometimes in imagination he stood in the dock and heard the boy stammering his story from the witness-box.

Sometimes he projected himself into the future, and the boy, grown into a man, recognised his father's assassin and took summary vengeance in a hundred different and ghastly ways. Once he woke up and heard himself mutter aloud:

'That kid'll be the death of me yet.'

His wife had roused and had asked sleepily:

'What kid?'

He stared at her, aghast, and then recovered his composure.

'That kid down at Simpson's who's always messing about with the Ford. Took the reed out of the 'ooter the other day. Nice thing that might have been for me—goin' round a corner.'

His superstition grew rather than diminished. If one of the women whom he had visited had any impediment of speech, or if she came to the door with a red-haired child clinging to her skirt, he was careful never to call at the same house again.

He prospered, and was outwardly happy, but the fear lingered and grew.

'That kid'll be the death of me yet. I know! I know!' And the sight of a policeman sauntering along a road, or standing at a comer with alert eyes for every passing face, still turned his heart to water. He knew the folly of his fears. He was safe now—safe except for that boy, who might not recognise him if they met face to face, and could prove nothing if he did.

It was on a summer afternoon, four and a half years after the Weybury murder, that Ernest Peckham returned home from his round early in the afternoon, to be greeted by his wife, who wore a portentous air of mystery.

'Policeman's been round to see you, Ern,' she announced.

He felt his jaw drop and his cheeks whiten.

'What does he want?' he jerked out.

'Not knowing, can't say. 'E didn't tell me, and it don't pay to ask questions. You ain't been stopped on the road, 'ave you? Your licence ain't run out, or anything?'

'No.' He felt suddenly sick and ill. 'No; everything's all in order.' He was thinking: 'That kid—he's spotted me and told! He'll be my death—that kid!'

'Well, you won't 'ave long to wait,' his wife continued. "'E'll be round again at four o'clock. I told 'im you'd be in by then.'

He turned upon her fiercely.

'Then you didn't ought to have told him anything of the sort. I shan't be in—see! I'm goin' out again. And when he comes round, you just ask him what it's all about—see!'

His wife laughed aloud.

'You are a fool, Ern,' she said, 'to get all 'ot and bothered over nothing. I believe I know what it is. 'E's 'erd you 'aven't took out a licence for the dog. That'll be seven-and-six, my lad, even if they don't fine you.' Peckham lurched towards the door.

'You find out what he wants,' he said. 'Ask him straight out, and then tell me.'

The Ford was still outside. He clambered in and drove away, with the sweat pouring off his forehead. That was it, undoubtedly—the dog licence. Only he could not bear the thought of being at home when the policeman came back, of enduring the moment or two which would elapse before the man stated his business. He was quite aware of the folly of driving away. If it were the Other Thing, he was already in worse case than a trapped rat. But his nerves would not let him stay.

He drove wildly, recklessly, scarcely noticing that he was heading straight for Weybury. But the thought would not have troubled him. He had done business in the town a hundred times in the last few years, choosing always those hours when he knew the children would be in school. They would still be in school; it wasn't four yet.

They came out even as he entered the outskirts of the town. A triangle on the left of the road, with a notice beneath it, warned him, and he slackened speed a little, but only a little. He was moving at thirty miles an hour when half a dozen boys ran out through an iron gateway, kicking a tennis ball into the road.

Half angrily and half desperately he snatched at the bulb of the horn. All save one of the boys started and leaped back on to the pavement. The last ran, stooping, to recover the ball. Down the road, on the other side, came humming a laden motor-coach.

For the second time in his life Ernest Peckham lost his head. On the first occasion he had taken life; this time he spared it at the greatest of all costs. He struck the charabanc almost bonnet to bonnet, and he died that night in the cottage hospital.

'I knew that kid 'ud be the death of me,' were the last words he muttered to the nurse. Knowing no better, she thought that he had made a deliberate and heroic choice. You may find on his tombstone the text beginning: 'Greater love hath no man'.

The boy who was the cause of the accident gave evidence at the inquest. The coroner was very kind to him, remembering a previous tragedy. He was a red-haired boy, named Gilkes, and he stammered painfully.

For One Night Only

I met old Sydney Hippett in The Griffin that Sunday evening. You know Sydney Hippett, the animal trainer, who, with his performing dogs and monkeys, has visited pretty near every music-hall in Britain? I was showing at the local Hip, for the coming week, and I'd just seen by the bill hanging up on the wall that Hippett was showing, too, when in he walked.

My own name doesn't matter, but I'm pretty well known to the public as Tom Gass, the Loquacious Comedian. I'm a good comedian, but no hand at writing a yarn. I shall have to tell it in my own way, and if that doesn't suit you, you needn't read it. After all, as Shakespeare didn't say, 'the story's the thing'.

I knew Hippett pretty well, or thought I did. We had a couple of drinks together, and he asked me where were my digs.

'Lottie Ludlow's down here,' he went on to say. 'You can see that by the bill, though. She's very sick because she can't find digs to suit her. Careless girl—Lottie. Never troubles about getting addresses while she's on tour. Simply blows down on a strange town and trusts to luck. Any room for her in your place?'

'I know there isn't,' I replied. 'I asked if they could fix up my pal, Gus Leyton, but the old ma told me she hadn't another vacant room in the place. By the way, Syd, you'd better come round for a bit of supper and a game of "vanty" or something. Gus is coming, and I've managed to wangle a dozen of Bass and a bottle of Black and White.'

'Thanks,' he answered, 'I've got nothing on. What's the address, though?'

'Forty-one, Tutbury Road—quite near the station.'

His hand shook, and he spilt half that remained of his glass of Bass over the counter.

'Not me,' he answered vehemently. 'Not in these! I've been there before! They know me in that house!'

Well, I didn't ask questions. We're not all saints in the profession, and I knew Syd was no better than most. There must have been a lot of houses about the country in which he daren't show his head. The funny thing was, though, that I hadn't noticed a pretty girl about the place; but then, I'd only been in it for an hour or two.

We didn't speak for a minute or so, and then he asked abruptly:

'Who put you on to those digs? You haven't stayed there before?'

'Never shown here before,' I answered, i got the address from Lily Ginetta. She said they were quite reasonable and did her very well.'

At that moment I received a terrific slap on the back, and there was my pal, Gus Leyton, standing grinning behind me. With him was Dicky Cobbold.

I daresay you've seen them on the halls. Gus is 'songs and imitations at the piano,' and Dicky kids the public that he's a ventriloquist.

'I've got fixed up,' said Gus. 'I'm with Dicky Cobbold. Not too bad a place. May I bring Dicky along with me tonight?'

'Do,' I answered, 'I asked Syd Hippett here, too, but he can't manage it.'

'Oh, he's a dirty dog!' Gus said, grinning. 'Always full up with engagements. How's the monkeys, Syd?'

'Still a dam sight better looking than you, and about twice as sensible,' he answered. With that he swallowed his drink, nodded to us, and walked out.

We all looked at each other and laughed when he'd gone.

'Queer fish, that,' Dicky said. 'Gets more and more unsociable.'

'Good animal trainer, though,' I said.

'Trains women pretty well, too,' said Gus. 'I've heard him talk to them, and heard the swish of the lash in his voice. Can't say I like the brute!'

Well, we'd all heard stories about Syd Hippett, but we weren't scandal-mongers, so we didn't start yarning. We had one more drink and then strolled along to my digs.

I had a bedroom and a sitting-room on the top floor but one, in a roomy old house which had seen better days before the old ma took it and let it out in lodgings for pros. It was a gloomy old place, but the rooms were large, and everything looked about as clean as one could expect.

The fire was burning up well when we arrived, and I lit the incandescent, and got out the bottles and glasses and a pack of cards.

'It wants about half-an-hour to the time I ordered supper,' I said, looking at the clock. 'Care for a game of something now to fill in the time? Nap or "vanty"?'

We agreed on 'vanty', cut for the bank, and I won. The very first hand I laid down a 'natural' and drew double stakes from both of them.

'Tom's luck!' said Gus. 'Always wins at cards. Always finds the best digs. Always'

'Yes, the digs are all right,' Dicky interrupted, 'so long as the ceiling doesn't come down while you're here.'

'Which it will,' said Gus, 'if the athlete overhead hops about like that very much longer.'

I looked up at the ceiling, which was full of cracks but looked safe enough for the time being. But overhead there was a soft bumping and thudding, which went on and on as if it never meant to stop. It did stop, while I was looking up, but went on again a few minutes later, it began to get on our nerves.

'What is that darned row?' exclaimed Dicky, who was then holding the bank. 'Did you say "twist?" Good, that's bust it! It isn't somebody up there with a hammer, is it?'

'Sounds more like some blithering idiot with a skipping-rope,' I said.

We all listened. Then Gus burst out laughing.

'Can't you tell what that is?' he asked, it's one of the pros practising a dance. Who's staying here besides you?'

'Don't know,' I answered.

'Well, who's doing a dancing act down here this week? Lottie Ludlow?'

'She's not here,' I answered, 'Syd Hippett told me she was looking for digs, and that was after ma had told me the place was full.'

'Well,' said Gus, puzzled. 'Who else is doing a dancing act at the Hip, this week? It's a girl, too. A man wouldn't be as light as that on his feet.'

'Oh, what does it matter?' Dicky said, dealing the cards. 'We can ask the old ma who it is when she brings up the supper. If it doesn't stop then, Tom, you can send her a kind message.'

Mrs Pringold arrived with the supper-tray about half-an-hour later.

During that half-hour the dancing overhead had been going on almost continuously. She was a thin woman, was Mrs Pringold, with almost a bluish tinge to her face—one of those women who always seem to be suffering from the cold. She hitched a dark shawl closer around her shoulders when she had put the tray on the table.

'It's easy to tell you've got a house full of pros, ma,' I said.

'Why?'

'Well, we can hear a premiere danseuse getting into training. You be careful she doesn't wear your linoleum out, ma.'

'And bring the ceiling down,' said Gus.

She looked at all three of us in turn. She seemed not to understand, but there was a queer look about her thin, cold face.

'Do you mean to say you can't hear somebody dancing?' Dicky exclaimed. 'There! Right overhead!'

She gave a quick glance up at the ceiling, and stood with her thin hands clasped, listening.

'I can hear something,' she said—and she'd have been deaf if she couldn't, it's the wind.'

'Wind! Rubbish!' I chipped in. it's somebody dancing or skipping. I don't mind it for a bit, but it'll have to stop sooner or later. Who's got the room overhead, ma?'

'Nobody,' she answered, turning towards the fire, it's an empty attic. Nobody's dancing there.'

'I thought you said you'd let all your rooms?' I said quickly.

'So I have—all I've got to let. I don't let that one. There's no furniture in it—not proper furniture. The wind often makes funny noises up there. The windows are all loose.'

'Let's go up and have a look,' I said, if that's not somebody jumping about I'll eat my hat.'

'The door's locked,' she answered. 'There can't be anybody there.'

Well, we had to let it go at that. As Gus said, the wind makes funny noises in old houses, and the old girl ought to know whether she'd got a dancing Dervish about the place or not. Then, while we were having supper the noise stopped, and it didn't break out again. I'd almost forgotten all about it by the time the two boys went.

They left me at half-past twelve, and at one I went to bed and fell asleep almost at once. At two—the luminous dial of my watch told me the time—I was broad awake again. I knew something had woke me and I hadn't to listen more than a moment to find out what it was.

The garret above must have been a long one, running the length of my bedroom and sitting room—I afterwards found out that it did, and there was the dancing, just above the ceiling, going on as merrily as ever.

Well, I'm not one of those who jib at a few inconveniences in lodgings. A chap must expect to have to put up with them. But to have somebody dancing overhead at two in the morning was a bit too thick. So I jumped up, put on slippers and a dressing-gown, and groped my way to the stairs. I was pretty wild and I meant that the dancing lady—I was sure it was a girl—should have a piece of my mind.

I heard the dancing plainer than ever when I got on to the landing above. It was as dark as the inside of a tiger, but I blundered against a door, while I was feeling for one, and knocked. I got no answer. Whoever was inside took no notice whatever.

I found the handle and turned it, and just as the door came open in my hand, I remembered the landlady having told me it was locked. 'Old liar!' I thought. And 'old liar!' I thought again at the sight which met my eyes.

The window was broken, and through the starred gash the wind came rushing. Beyond I could see the moon and thin white clouds racing across it. And between me and the window a girl in a short dancing skirt pirouetted on her toes, holding out with both hands the ends of a long emerald-green cape.

She wore a little emerald-green bonnet, her short skirt was slashed with green, her shoes and stockings were white. Her face seemed very white, but I couldn't see it plainly because her back was towards what little light there was. But I thought—you know how quickly thoughts come into one's head—how like she was to Kitty O'Carr, a little comedienne and dancer I'd played with years ago. Her Irish get-up and dance was a crib on Kitty O'Carr's 'business'.

I only saw her for a matter of seconds, for a sudden gust of wind wrenched the door handle out of my hand and slammed the door in my face. Well, I didn't open it again. I simply called through the chink:

'Do give it a rest tonight, my dear. Some of us want to get some sleep.'

She did stop then and I went downstairs. I thought of asking her if she were Kitty, but I didn't. It wasn't the time or the place for talking, and I could find out easy enough next day. But when I got into bed again and started to think, I was a bit puzzled by things.

In the first place I couldn't understand a girl hopping about like that for hours on end without music. And I couldn't understand what had made the girl take a room with a broken window and hardly any furniture. And I couldn't for the life of me think why ma had denied there was anybody there, unless she was ashamed of letting such a room to a pro.

Then I started thinking of Kitty. Was it Kitty who had that room? I hadn't seen her for years. Somehow she seemed to have dropped out suddenly. I'd meant to inquire what had become of her, but always forgotten. It's not a bit unusual for a girl who's doing quite well in the profession to drop right out suddenly and never be heard of again.

In the end I decided that it couldn't be Kitty. At least, her name wasn't on the bills, and she always used to go on as a single turn. I made up my mind I'd find out who it was next morning, decided that ma was a 'holy friar', and went to sleep.

Next morning, after breakfast, I ran upstairs and knocked at that attic door. As nobody answered me I opened it and looked in, and I saw at a glance that nobody could have lived in that room for years. The place was thick with dust, and I should imagine I'd been dreaming the night before if I hadn't seen the broken window and the few broken-down sticks of furniture.

I determined to say nothing to ma just then. Very likely she'd let the girl use the room to practise dancing, and denied that she'd done so to me, because I was objecting to the noise. But there was something very queer and unusual about the whole thing, and ma's manner had seemed very strange. I was bound to spot the girl at that afternoon's rehearsal, and, if she lived in some other part of the house, I made up my mind to walk home with her, confront ma with her, and say: 'What about the wind in the attic now?' or words to that effect.

That Monday afternoon's rehearsal was like any other Monday afternoon show. There was the usual grumbling over the order of the turns. The orchestra went through everybody's band-parts, and we came on and did part of a turn each to empty seats. But I didn't see the girl I'd seen dancing in the attic. Lottie Ludlow was the only dancing act, and she was a great fat girl who clattered about in clogs.

After I'd been on and managed to knock some sense into the conductor's head, I was standing in the wings talking to Gus and Dicky. I couldn't understand the business about that dancing girl, and I was beginning to feel a bit creepy over it. She couldn't have been 'on' anywhere else, as the Hippodrome was the only theatre in the town. I was thinking of the little Irish girl who used to sing and dance, and who looked like the girl I'd seen last night. So I turned round quite suddenly to Gus and said:

'By the way, what has become of Kitty O'Carr?'

The words were no sooner out of my mouth than I heard an oath behind me, and Syd Hippett pushed Gus and Dicky out of the way and planted himself in front of me.

'Do you want me to knock your ugly little head off?' he asked.

I didn't. And as Syd was about twice my size I couldn't have stopped him. I thought at first he was spoofing, and you could have knocked me over with a feather, I was so surprised. So I said: 'Keep your hair on, Syd. I'm not one of your monkeys.'

'Yes, you're beastly funny, aren't you?' he sneered. 'You be careful what you say and what names you mention, or I'll smash you!'

The others got in between us then, and told Syd not to be a fool, and pushed him away. And there was I, quite innocent of any intention to annoy him, and wondering what on earth I'd said that was out of place.

'You see,' Gus whispered to me a minute or two later, 'he thought you knew he was standing behind us, and I suppose he jumped to the conclusion that you were talking at him.'

'Talking at him! I asked what had become of Kitty O'Carr. How could I have been talking at him?'

'Don't pretend you don't know,' Gus said. 'You must remember. Everybody knows. By gum, I believe it happened in this very town, too!'

'Yes, it did happen here,' Dicky said gravely.

'What did?' I asked.

They both looked at me in bewilderment. Then Dicky said:

'It must have happened while you were doing that twelve months' tour in Canada and the States.'

'Ten years ago?'

'Yes, about then.'

'Well, what happened?'

'Syd Hippett was supposed to be going to marry Kitty O'Carr. She died in her digs somewhere in the town here, and Syd had to attend the inquest—that's all. Hullo! You're looking pretty queer all of a sudden.'

I leaned up against the electrician's ladder.

'I feel queer,' I said. 'You don't happen to have a flask of brandy on you, do you?'

An hour later I'd found some new digs, and went round to collect my props from the old ones.

'I'm sorry to leave you,' I told the old woman, 'I'm not very particular about my rooms. I can put up with half-cold food, the cat eating my supper, rats, mice, and hard mattresses. But I draw the line at ghosts.'

She stared at me and fell back a step. Her cold-looking face went white, and her straight mouth dropped at the corners.

'You won't tell the others?' she said in a whisper. 'You won't ruin me?'

'I get called a liar quite often enough without spinning a yarn like this,' I told her.

'Besides, there's no ghost there,' she said, recovering herself. 'That noise you heard was made by the wind. I've been up to that attic a hundred times at night and seen nothing.'

'I've only been once,' I said, with a shiver, 'and I wasn't so lucky. And now, before I go, I want to know how Kitty O'Carr came to die in that room.

You needn't tell me she didn't, because I know she did.'

She looked at me for a moment as if she couldn't speak. Then at last she said: 'if you won't tell the others'

'The others all know,' I told her, 'but I want to hear from you.'

'They found out afterwards that she had a bad heart. The shock'

'Begin at the beginning, please.'

'Oh, I suppose you know it all already,' she said wearily. 'Miss O'Carr had my big top room, the one I haven't let since. She was playing down here the same week as Mr Hippett. They were engaged. One night, home she comes from the theatre in high spirits, her turn having gone even better than usual. She'd come home in her stage clothes, make-up and all, with a water-proof over them. And so happy and light-hearted she was that she started doing one of her dances for me when I took up her supper tray. While she was jigging about the room, up comes the girl—I kept one then—with a note. It was from Mr Hippett. She took it from me and opened it and read it while she danced.

'Then, down she flopped on the floor, poor thing, and never moved again. She died dancing, as you might say. The note from Mr Hippett was read at the inquest, and a cruel note it was. It told her that he was going to marry some other woman; and I suppose she'd have been well shut of him, but girls don't look at these things in that light. The coroner said that her heart was in such a bad state—though perhaps she didn't know it—that she oughtn't to have danced at all, and the least shock was likely to send her off. That's all there is to tell you. It happened close upon ten years ago, as perhaps you've heard.'

And that's about all there is to it, as they say. I'm a comedian, and I don't profess to be able to tell stories—not this kind of story.

Syd Hippett is still touring the halls with his performing animals, and I'd sooner be dead than be any dog or monkey trained by him. He's a strong man and a brave man in a way, but there's one set of digs that he daren't set foot in. And, unless you're looking for trouble, don't mention to him the name of Kitty O'Carr, or the address of the house I slept in for one night only.

The Case of Thissler and Baxter

I knew all about Thissler's recurring or, rather, continuous dreams, for he had often told me about them. Indeed, unless carefully handled, he was apt to become wearying, like any other man who is always anxious to revert to one particular topic of conversation concerning himself.

The first time he told me about his dream existence as Mr Baxter, I now dare frankly confess that I didn't believe him. I thought he had invented it all with the purpose of becoming an object of half amusing, half uncanny interest.

'Directly I go to sleep,' he said, I become an altogether different man, and live in an altogether different place. I am a short paunchy man of fifty-five, a corn merchant, and I live in a small town called Thurlbury. My name is Baxter, and I am a big pot in a small way. I am an alderman and I have twice been mayor. I am married to a thin insipid woman of rather limited intelligence, and I have two grown-up daughters, Ethel and Clara. It is all as real to me as is my ordinary existence as Charles Thissler, stockbroker's clerk.'

'Do you mean to say,' I asked, 'that you dream this every night?'

'I don't think you understand,' he replied, 'I don't dream the same dream over again. Directly I fall asleep I *am* Alderman Baxter, and simply live through the ordinary petty details of his daily life. Nothing exciting or important ever happens. Our occasional family quarrels are very mild. I am perpetually rebuking Ethel for being fast, and Clara for her temper. I am pretty well off, and not a little self-satisfied. It is only when I wake up as Thissler that I realise that, as Baxter, I am a pretty dull sort of dog.'

'I've never heard of anything so extraordinary,' I murmured, far too polite to call a bigger man than myself a liar.

'Nor have I. The dreams go on in an unbroken chain. Directly I fall asleep each night I go on where I left off on waking. I've been wondering lately if there is such a man as Baxter or such a town as Thurlbury. In my dreams it's a potty little place of about five thousand people, somewhere in the Midlands.'

'Look it up in the ABC,' I suggested. 'There's sure to be a station there.'

'Right, I will,' he said. 'And if there should turn out to be an Alderman Baxter, corn merchant of that town, I shall hand myself over to the Society of Psychic Research to see what they can make of me.'

'Are the dreams as vivid as your waking life?' I inquired.

'Absolutely.'

'Then you must wonder whether you're really asleep or awake—whether you're really Thissler or Baxter. And you can't be both?'

'Ah,' he returned, 'I thought you were going to say that. But I know I'm awake now, and really Thissler, because when I'm Baxter I have no recollection of being Thissler. But really it amounts to this—I get no real sleep at all, I simply go on with another man's life.'

I had to laugh then, but I soon checked myself as I saw that he was ruffled.

'Do you know anything at all about corn and oats and dried peas and that sort of thing?' I inquired.

He laughed in his turn.

'My dear man, as Baxter I'm a bally authority. Only my knowledge doesn't pass out of the dream with me. I know all this must sound perfectly incredible to you. But if it doesn't— what do you make of it?'

I made the usual fatuous jokes about drink and late suppers and left him. His story recurred to my mind two days later when I was looking up a train to Swindon. I was hastily looking through the ABC, and naturally came to the T's before the S's. And suddenly, as I was in the act of turning some pages, the name Thurlbury caught my eye.

Thurlbury, it seemed, was in Warwickshire, and had a population of 6,410. I was a little surprised to see it until I had thought the matter over. Then it occurred to me that Thissler, if he had invented the story about his dreams, would naturally have made it as circumstantial as possible by preparing the details first. It would not have surprised me to find that there was a Baxter, corn merchant of that town, who was also an alderman. There are such things in directories.

A week later I ran across Thissler once more, and being reminded of his extraordinary story, told him that the town of Thurlbury actually existed. I know it does,' he said, a gleam of excitement in his eyes. 'I took your tip and looked it up. As soon as I can spare a day off I'm going down there, and if I can find such a man as Baxter I'm going to introduce myself to him. Wouldn't it be extraordinary if, as soon as he goes to sleep, he becomes *me!*'

We both laughed at the far-fetched absurdity of the idea, but there was a note of seriousness in his tone.

'How are Clara and Ethel?' I inquired.

'Oh, quite fit, thanks,' he answered with a grin. 'But just before I woke up this morning I had to give Ethel a pretty healthy wigging for going to the pictures with a man who hadn't been properly introduced to her. Can you beat it?'

I said I couldn't and wasn't going to try. And thereafter he formed a habit of sidling up to me and telling me half seriously, half in amusement, all that Mrs Baxter and Ethel and Clara had been doing. As I have already stated, it began to bore me after a time, and consequently I avoided him as much as possible. He was very busy in those days, and was continually expressing his regret at being unable to steal the time to pay a visit to Thurlbury. It must have been five or six weeks after he first told me of the strange affair when one evening he came round to my place looking white and haggard.

'I want you to do me a favour,' he said—'a pretty big one. I want you to sit up with me all night, play chess, cards, any old thing, drink black coffee, and stop me from going to sleep.'

'Why on earth?' I demanded.

'Because I daren't. Last night I had my usual continuation of the same dream, and as Baxter I fell down in my shop in a sort of fit. I simply can't tell you how perfectly horrible I felt. They carried me to bed and fetched a doctor. I overheard him tell my wife—I mean Mrs Baxter, of course—that I couldn't live for more than a few hours. I didn't feel like it either. So, don't you see?—I simply daren't go to sleep tonight and continue that dream.'

There was no mistaking the man's sincerity, although I tried to laugh away his terrors.

'Why,' I said, 'if you dreamed again tonight you'd only *dream* that you died.'

'I won't risk it!' he said hoarsely.

I knew now, by his whole manner, that this dream-story of his was not a piece of conscious invention on his part. And although I thought his fears were shadowy, I am a humane man who can sympathise with another's terrors. I was never a glutton for sleep, but although I like my small share, I willingly agreed to sit up all night with him and keep him awake.

It was about the dullest night I ever spent. I hate draughts and chess and such card games as two can play. Thissler dared not read nor permit me to read. And so we swilled black coffee and played interminable games of chess which would have disgraced children of seven. At last came the merciful dawn, and breakfast, and we parted company, I to bed, and he to the office, looking wan and hollow-eyed.

The following morning he was round at my place before breakfast, his eyes staring with excitement, his cheeks and forehead flushed.

'Well,' I said, 'did you venture on some sleep last night?'

'I did,' he answered, 'and I didn't dream a thing. You'll know why when you've seen this. Look!'

He had with him a copy of the *Daily Wire* open in the middle and then folded twice across. He pointed at a column split into very small news paragraphs, and I looked where his thumbnail dug into the paper.

'*Alderman Baxter,*' I read, '*a corn merchant of Thurlbury, and twice mayor of that borough, died at his residence early yesterday morning after a brief illness. He will be remembered for much philanthropic work in connection with his native town.*'

The words seemed to lose themselves in a haze under my eyes.

'Good Lord!' I said softly. 'This is beyond everything I've ever hear of!'

'I wonder,' said Thissler, his eyes suddenly moistening with awe—'I wonder what would have happened to me if I'd gone to sleep that night?'

The Witch Of Oxshott

It is strange how old the world has grown since first I knew it, and what tools this generation has produced. The young whelps, proud of their store of learning, have created new philosophies in place of those which served their forbears. They are pink and white, over-dressed Sadducees. And we old men, who have not the time nor the strength to be angry, listen to them and smile in patience.

Only t'other day a young man told me that he believed only what he saw, and I had an answer ready for him, for the gift of using my tongue remains with me. What could he have seen, poor little cub, fresh from its mother?

And 'tis so with many of them. They will not believe there is a hell until their fat is frizzling.

Last Sunday our parson, a man of parts and extensive learning, preached a sermon on superstition, and chided the village-folk for their belief in witchcraft, and it troubled me to see that so admirable a man had forgotten the Witch of Endor and one of the Laws of Moses. I have since spoken nothing to him on the subject, nor shall; but I have seen what I have seen, and during the rest of his discourse I closed my eyes and slipped back into the Past, so that that scene in the lonely house returned to me with all its haunting horror.

'Twas in those days when I, Captain Jack Bishop, outlaw and toby-man, roamed the highways with a price upon my head, picking my living in a way that would have grieved my mother, had she lived to see it; and 'twas late in the winter of 1748 that what I am about to set down took place.

I had done well on the York Road, and made it too hot to hold me. A friendly innkeeper warned me that the narks were hot on my track, so I retreated quietly and made my way south of London, through Hertfordshire and Middlesex. I had intended going as far south as Hayward's Heath before starting business once more, but while slaking my thirst at The Greyhound at Leatherhead I read a bill offering a reward for my capture, which lessened my anxiety. 'Twas the most unfaithful and unflattering description of me possible to conceive; but I was not unthankful to its author. I was in no more danger from it than a village curate, so I decided to take my leisure and sleep the night in Dorking.

There was the very faintest touch of frost in the air, and as there had been a spell of dry weather the roads made travelling a pleasure. The moon was up, and in her third quarter, and the stars burnt brightly in a clear sky.

I bestrode Meg with a lightsome heart, and gloried in the rhythm of our progress and the rush of cold wind in my face; and though the starlight and the whispering trees that lined the road bade me dream awhile of the maid, Barbara, who had gone out of my life for ever, 'twas too fresh a night for a man to carry a sore heart in his body.

'Faith, I had not nearly reached Dorking when the pangs of hunger assailed me, and I began to cast about me for the sight of a friendly inn wherein I might appease them.

I found one in a little hollow under the shadow of the downs. 'Twas in a little village, the name of which, if my memory serves me, was Mickleham. I remember it as a scattering of tiny cottages built at crazy angles on the pine-clad hillside, some of them with gardens on a slope, like the face of a cliff.

There was a small inn there facing the iron gates of a gentleman's house. I think 'twas named The Acorn. 'Twas devilish small, and the ostler, who came out in answer to my summons, told me that there was no room for Meg in the stable.

'Her master will not feed unless she does,' says I. 'So take her into the yard and feed and water her. I leave here the moment I have supped.'

With that I strode into the house and demanded the coffee-room. A loud-voiced doxie showed it me, and I found 'twas little better than a tap-room, with benches and a plain deal table on trestles. I therefore decided to eat but sparingly, and allay the pangs of hunger until I reached Dorking, where I could sup as a gentleman should.

The wench informed me that the house contained no better fare than cold bacon and pickles, and made some attempt to be insolent when she saw my wry face. I called for a clay pipe, and filled and lit it while she laid the table.

Now it was the last house in Christendom where I should have expected to see gentlemen foregather, and I was vastly astonished when two men, whose dress and bearing proclaimed them to be gentlemen of some breeding, strode into the room where I was seated, and, wishing me 'Good evening!' threw themselves on to a settle in front of the fire and asked for ale.

Although dissimilar in features, they were both young and of the same height, build, and colouring, so that a description of one might serve equally well for the other. Their red faces, and the space between their knees as they walked, told me that they were country-bred and used to riding.

I noticed that they gave me many curious glances, and after a while one of them addressed me.

'A stranger, sir?' says he, courteously enough.

I bowed in assent. ''Twere easy to guess that, seeing the house you find me in,' says I; at which they laughed.

' 'Tis hospitable enough when you come to know it,' remarked the other.

'There is no better brew in Surrey, and the house is open to us at all hours of the day and night. If you are like to be here tomorrow, sir, I can promise you sport, for I have a game-cock which I have backed to the tune of a hundred pounds against a bird which my friend, Mr Gilbert Cross, here, will set against him.'

'I shall be sorry to miss it,' says I, 'but I am bound for Brighton.'

At that point the wench came in with the cold bacon, exchanged a jest with Mr Gilbert Cross and his friend, and invited me to be seated at the table.

'A great traveller?' Mr Cross said, as I fell to work with my knife and fork.

'I have seen some of the world,' I answered, 'and most of England. You gentlemen are to be congratulated. You live in a favoured spot.'

'Ay,' says Mr Cross, 'the land is comely enough, but dull.' He rapped out an oath, adding: 'Dull is not the word.'

His friend chuckled, and broke a half-burn log on the fire with his heel.

'We should rot like wet hay if the devil sent us nothing to do,' he laughed.

'We have naught to do, sir, but sit still and wait to don our fathers' shoes. They're godly men, both of them, and fear to allow us to enter the larger world because of its vast temptations.'

I laughed at that, for I had learned that the devil is sometimes busier in a village than in the heart of a city.

'If 'twere not for the maids we should go mad,' says Mr Cross. 'You have seen the world, sir: confess that you must come to Surrey to find a pretty wench. George Tressilly here agrees with me. And he has seen the maids of the North, besides those of London and Brighton.'

'Oh, they are well enough,' I answered, desiring to be agreeable. 'For me, I take but little notice of them.'

'A little notice,' says Mr Cross, 'is all that a man need take. The man who lays his heart before a maid will have it trampled on. 'Tis a match between them - '

'Ay,' Mr Tressilly interrupted. 'And when the woman loses she pays heavily. Which reminds me,' he added, glancing at Mr Cross, 'that naught has been heard of Mildred Garland, who left her home at Oxshott these three months since. Had you given her all your heart, friend Cross, you would have been sighing and moping like—like -'

'Like young Stephen Tenterden,' laughed Cross. ''Tis a fair illustration of what I have been saying. Tenterden set her in a shrine, and she laughed at him; he laid his heart before her, and she trod it into the dirt; he offered her all he possessed, and she turned from him in scorn.'

'And you,' Tressilly laughed, 'offered her little enough, and she took less and loved you. That is the way of women.'

Now it seemed to me that Mr Cross was growing a trifle uneasy, for he shifted his position and frowned slightly at his friend.

'Nay,' he replied, 'she loved me not. There was but the merest acquaintance between us. I saw her but half-a-dozen times, and she pleased me little.'

Now Mr Tressilly's face assumed the half-surprised, half-amused look of a man who has heard an amazing lie. He seemed about to speak, and then checked himself, perchance on account of my presence.

At that moment we heard the sound of a galloping horse, and Mr Cross craned forward and peered through the window.

'Gad!' he cried. 'We have spoken of the devil, and here he is! 'Tis Stephen Tenterden.'

I heard the man outside dismount, and presently the sound of heavy boots stamping on the hollow floor. The door was thrown open and a young man, booted and spurred, strode into the room. The men on the settle hailed him, but he took no notice until he had flung off the heavy cape which he had worn round his shoulders. He was a young man of much the same type as Mr Tressilly and Mr Cross, but his face was as white as the ceiling had been before the smoke had stained it. His features were stern, angry, full of suffering; his nostrils were dilated and his lips drawn in, so that his mouth was a straight slit.

'Why, man,' cried Mr Cross, sitting bolt upright, 'what ails you?'

'That I have come to tell you,' Mr Tenterden answered sternly. 'They told me I should be like to find you here. First, I have news for you.'

'For us?' Tressilly repeated.

'It concerns Cross more closely than yourself,' the other replied. 'And for that you shall presently be thankful.'

There was silence for a moment. Mr Cross's face had turned a dingy grey. For my part, I held my breath and listened with all my ears, for I knew that the grim presence of tragedy overshadowed the room. Presently Mr Tenterden went on speaking, and the words came with an obvious effort. 'Mildred Garland came home yesterday.'

Mr Tressilly glanced nervously across at his friend. Mr Cross watched the speaker's face as one fascinated.

'She came home yesterday—in trouble. She died today.'

'My God!' Mr Tressilly whimpered. 'Cross'

Mr Cross pulled himself together with an effort. ' 'Tis a grievous thing,' he said shakily. 'But perhaps 'tis for the best. A woman who is neither maid nor wife is better where none may point at her.'

'You hound!' Tenterden burst out. 'You are the man!'

Mr Cross leaped to his feet with an oath as Tenterden sprang at him. The table before which I was seated was overturned, and went down with a crash. Mr Tressilly sprang between the two, who stood glaring across at each other, fingering the hilts of their swords.

'You lie!' cried a harsh voice, which I hardly recognised.

'Before she died she told us the name of the man—her mother and I. Yes, I was there, and if ever hate sent a soul to hell our curses have damned you. soul and body, too. Draw, you scoundrel—draw!'

Mr Tressilly remained stationary between the two men.

'No, no!' he cried. 'There shall be no fighting. 'Twould be murder—murder most foul! Cross is no swordsman.'

I got upon my legs and climbed over the fallen table.

'Mr Tressilly,' says I, 'it seems to me that there is a just quarrel between these gentlemen. Therefore, it ill befits you to stand between them. Let them fight it out. if you stand in their way I have a sword of my own, which you shall find sharper than yours.'

I saw at once that Mr Tressilly liked not the look of me, for he backed a step on to the hearth.

if it must be, it must be,' says he. 'But, for the sake of our host, let them fight outside.'

''Tis all one to me,' says Tenterden; and then turning to me: 'I thank you, sir. And I pray you keep an eye on that spawn of the devil, lest he escape.' Tenterden held the door for me to pass out first, and I was half across the threshold when I heard a loud scream behind me, which froze my blood and caused me to spring suddenly round; and were I to live through all the ages I should never forget the sight my eyes encountered.

Mr Cross was writhing and clawing at the air. All in an instant his face had changed from deathly white to a horrible red, the colour of live coals. A torrent of sweat was pouring from him.

Mr Tressilly seized him under the arms with a loud cry of 'Gilbert! Gilbert!' But he, blaspheming, tore himself free and wallowed on the floor, I am in hell!' he cried. 'Oh God, save me, save me! In hell!'

We all three watched him, trembling like men smitten with ague. I had seen horrors, but nothing like unto this. I was watching a man enduring the tortures of the damned, while yet his body and soul remained together. in hell—in hell!' he screamed; and as I watched him, sick at heart, I was conscious of others rushing past me into the room—the ostler, the serving wench, and a man whom I supposed must have been the landlord.

Mr Tressilly looked across at me and made his voice heard above the stricken man's screams.

'A surgeon!' he cried. 'For God's sake, a surgeon!'

Tenterden laughed hoarsely. 'A surgeon!' he echoed. 'Yes, fetch one. Fetch all the surgeons in the land, and they shall avail him nothing. This is the Judgment of God.'

Then the tortured man raised himself on his elbows and shrieked at me. 'Mrs Garland—tell her to cease! For the love of God tell her to cease. Tell her'

The voice became incoherent, and then a series of piercing cries burst from his lips.

I turned on my heel, swayed, and staggered through the doorway. I had seen enough. I wanted air, and open country, and the vault of heaven overhead. But the man's screams followed me into the road and into the stable yard, where I found Meg. I mounted her and sought out the village surgeon, telling him that a man lay grievously stricken at the inn. But I knew that I brought him forth on a fruitless errand.

Then, instead of riding into Dorking, as had been my intention. I turned Meg's head and set her galloping the way we had come, for the stricken man had given me a sort of message for Mrs Garland, who lived in the village of Oxshott, and I had a mind to deliver it.

At Leatherhead I stopped and inquired my way, and learned that Oxshott lies in the midst of the Crown woods, in the middle of the base of a triangle, of which the other two sides are the Portsmouth and Brighton roads, and the apex, Kingston.

'Twas not a long ride, but the way led through wild, weird country; and now I am old I take no shame to admit that a thousand terrors stalked me, and reached out shadowy hands to clutch me. To me, it seemed that something nameless and horrible kept pace with us in the darkness, and once, when Meg shied, I whipped out my pistols and stared about me as fearful as the veriest coward that ever dared travel by night.

In these country villages the people are early abed, and I found Oxshott as still as a churchyard. However, I had the fortune to meet one fellow returning home late from the woods—a poacher, as I should have guessed—and he told me where Mrs Garland lived, and looked strangely at me as he answered my inquiry. 'Twas not a peasant's house that I had to seek; 'twas a little square stone country house of about nine rooms, standing in an acre or more of garden—the kind of house where retired army officers and suchlike take up their abode.

I tethered Meg to the railing outside the gate and hurried up the short drive towards a row of white steps. There was no light in the hall, for the fanlight showed black above the door, but in a window on the first storey I could see a faint flickering illumination that grew and died away as gently and regularly as the swell of the sea.

I beat upon the door, and presently heard light footsteps and the sound of someone sobbing. The door was pulled open with a jerk, and a boy of twelve stood facing me across the threshold, with a rushlight in his clenched hand and molten tallow dripping and congealing on his fingers. His face was white, and his features swollen with grief, and his eyes, as he looked up at me, were deep wells of nameless horror.

That scene was terrible enough; the dim outlines of dingy furniture in the wide hall, and the boy with a nameless fear in his eyes, who seemed ready to drop, fainting, at every tick of the great clock that was beating somewhere out of sight. I was ever sensitive to the presence of things beyond the reach of my numbered senses, and I knew that I was within touch of something ghoulish and bizarre, of something that should be whispered of rather than spoken aloud. This feeling of mine is ill-described, but let that pass. Worse was to come.

The boy stammered some question in a sibilant undertone, and ere I could ask him to repeat what he had said, for I had not heard, the sound of laughter from some upper chamber broke on my ears.

I did not know at first if it were the laughter of a man, or of a woman, or of a devil. I should think 'twere just such a laugh as a lost soul hears as it leaves the body. Then a voice shouted in soft, sweet, silky, horrible tones:

'Is that Mr Gilbert Cross? Has he come at last?'

'I have a message from him,' I muttered.

The boy half-turned his head, and shouted in a quavering voice: 'No, mother. It is not he, but a gentleman who brings a message from him.'

Now I was a strong man, and had seen more of the rough side of the world than most, but I shuddered at the anticipation of again hearing that woman's voice; and when she answered her son, bidding him show me up, my flesh contracted as if I had touched some loathsome reptile.

'The second room on the left,' whispered the boy. 'Go you up alone, sir, for I dare not come with you.'

A desire to fly surged over me, and I made the greatest effort of my life when I entered and mounted those stairs. I knocked at a door, and the same voice that had called down bade me to enter. I pushed open the door and went in.

It was a large bedroom, lit only by the fire and a single candle—so badly lit, that I only saw its horrors one by one. Facing the door as I entered was a blazing fire, and before this a woman was crouching. Such light as there was, was all behind her, but as I stood between the jamb and the door, she moved the candle from the mantelpiece to a small table by her side. Then I saw her face, and was hard put to it to choke back the cry that strove to burst from my lips.

It was the face of a handsome woman of middle-age, but there was something in her eyes and the set of her features that was as foul and horrible as it is impossible to describe. She was like the incarnation of everything that is wicked, and I knew, as I looked at her, that this was black sin dwelling in the husk of a woman.

She smiled at me, and then allowed her eyes to wander. I followed their direction.

To the right of the door was a bed, on which someone was lying. The curtains were drawn back, and as I came farther into the room I could see the upturned marble face of a dead girl.

The woman by the fire laughed very softly.

'Yes. Look at her closely,' she said, in her horrible, silky voice. 'What you see is the work of Mr Gilbert Cross. Did you say, sir, that he gave you some message for me?'

'Madam,' says I, 'he was stricken suddenly by a strange and terrible malady, and he sends word, begging you to cease. To cease what, I do not know.'

'Ay, but he does.'

Then I saw that she was holding something in her hand. She looked up at me and leered horribly. Then, plucking a needle from her gown, she stabbed that which she was holding again and again, laughed aloud, and then rested it on the hot bars of the grate.

I took three short steps forward to look. Then I saw what is was, and my brain reeled. I had heard before of women who had sold their souls to the Powers of Evil to wreak vengeance on a man, making little effigies in wax of he whom they wished to torment. As the effigy is treated, so does the original sufferer.

I saw, squatting on the bars of the grate, a little wax image half-melted away. But its features were scarcely defaced, and I saw in them a repulsive likeness to those of Gilbert Cross.

'What devil's work is this?' I cried.

' 'Tis devil's work, surely enough,' she answered. 'Ay, the devil is sometimes good to us weak women. He gives us so much in exchange for our souls! And to call him to your aid is easy enough. You have but to burn a paste, made of the nails of a dead trollop, the blood of a maid.'

'Stop!' I cried, and shouted so that I need not hear her voice.

'I used my own daughter's nails,' she continued, in a voice that was horribly calm. 'Look at her—there she is! A good girl enough until she met Gilbert Cross and forgot her name, and drove her mother into the mire of hell. Ah!' She stooped suddenly and plucked the sweating wax from the bars with a pair of tongs. 'He must not die yet—not yet!'

That same instant I threw myself on her.

'Give that to me!' I shrieked.

She tried to elude me, and went down with a crash among the fire-irons. I had fallen, too, in my effort to seize her, and ere I could stretch out my hand for the tongs she had thrust them and what they contained into the blaze. A great flame sprang up, and shadows vanished from the walls and ceiling. I picked myself up, gasping for breath.

The woman pointed at the flame with a long forefinger. I remember that her hand was white and shapely and blue-veined.

'He is dying—dying!' she laughed. And then, staring at me with wild eyes, she began to cry obscene curses. 'The end is too soon!' I remember her shouting. 'He should have suffered for days—weeks. Mildred, my girl—look, look! There is the last of Gilbert Cross.'

She picked herself up, ran to the bed, and lifted the dead girl in her arms, turning the white face towards the dying flame.

I have a dim memory of the light changing to darkness, of feeling my way to the stairs, of falling down them, of dashing out wildly into God's own sweet air. My first clear recollection is of unhitching Meg's reins from the railings, springing on to her back, and riding away like a man possessed. I seldom used whip or spur, but I rode her like a devil that night, poor lass! I can remember little of that ride. I only know that I shouted at times to persuade myself that I was alive and awake. I know, too, that as we took the sharp turn in Leatherhead at a pace that no sane man would have ridden, faces came to the windows and looked down on us; and once I heard cries of 'Stop thief!' and 'Highwayman!'

Meg was dead beat 'ere we reached Mickleham, and we entered the village at little more than a walk.

The door of The Acorn was open, and ahead of me I saw lights and dark figures walking slowly, and heard the stumbling footfalls of men who bore a burden. A minute later I came abreast of Mr Tressilly, who recognised my voice when I addressed him.

'All's over,' he muttered, in a trembling voice. 'For God's sake don't look at his face!'

'I have not the wish,' I answered, and a fit of shuddering seized me.

'He died half an hour ago,' Mr Tressilly continued, 'in the bitterest torments it is possible to conceive. God alone knows how. The surgeon is at a loss.'

And I, who knew all, dropped behind that ghastly procession and, in the darkness, I made the sign of the Cross.

The Fourth Wall

When Forran complained of pains in the head, a steadily declining appetite, and a growing difficulty in getting to sleep, his wife urged him to waste no more faith on the local practitioner and spend two guineas on a visit to some great man in Harley Street. And after two months of gentle bullying, and a miserable consciousness of growing worse instead of better, Forran went.

The Harley Street doctor earned his two guineas in as many minutes. When Forran left the house he found himself pledged to give up work for at least two months, and rest in some quiet and bracing part of the country. Forran was one of three partners in a firm of solicitors, and as he was not a poor man it was not difficult for him to arrange for an eight or nine weeks holiday. His idea was to take a furnished cottage within easy distance of some pike fishing, and where rough shooting might also be obtained. Mrs Forran was to accompany him.

At first, their plan was to go away by themselves, but it occurred to Forran that such an arrangement might be very dull for poor Betty, and Mrs Forran thought that a little company other than her own might be good for dear Jack. Thus it came about that Tom and Helen Marriott, Mrs Forran's brother and sister, were urged to join them.

At that time I was just beginning to realise that life without Helen would be worse than a lingering death; so I angled tactfully for an invitation, which eventually I received from Mrs Forran, who saw how it was with me. So we went away five strong, a happy little party, whose members could be relied upon to live for two months under the same roof without wearing upon each other.

Jack Forran saw the advertisement of the furnished cottage in a weekly paper devoted to such things, and Tom went down into Huntingdonshire to look at it. He returned full of ecstasies. He had never seen such a cottage, he said; and in five minutes we had caught his enthusiasm. It was very old, and had been endowed with the comforts of civilisation without losing its antiquity. It was furnished throughout with genuine old furniture, and the whole place contained nothing shoddy and not one jarring note. In a word, it was the cottage one often dreams of but seldom sees.

For the rest, Tom had to admit that it was miles from any town or village, but he argued that this seclusion was just what we wanted. Moreover, the Great Ouse was only half an hour's walk distant, and there, he told us, the wildfowl were crying aloud to be shot and the pike begging to be caught. So Jack, without wasting time, wrote to the London agent, and took this paragon of cottages for two months, antique furniture and all.

We arrived on a December evening, having driven five miles in a slow trap from a little village station on the branch line from Cambridge. Our cottage stood just outside the region of the fens, but it had been built on the crest of what passes for a hill in that part of the country, and Tom guaranteed it to be fairly dry. In other respects we were prepared for disappointments, for we had begun to fear that he had made us expect too much. We got ready to fall upon him and find fault.

But when the door was opened to us, and one after another we crossed the threshold into a warm room flooded with soft light, we were all ready to swear that Tom had done the place less than justice.

The door opened straight into the one large living-room, and opposite to us a grandfather's clock ticked loudly and with elderly precision. On our right hand logs were burning on the wide, open hearth, in the ingles of which were chintz-covered seats. Already I fancied myself there with Helen, we two alone in the firelight, watching the grey smoke curling up into the wide chimney. Heavy beams supported the low ceiling, and one ran diagonally along the cream-washed wall, sloping downwards from the ceiling and disappearing behind the clock.

Beside the clock were two doors, one leading to the kitchen and the other to the stairs. There was another door on our left as we entered, and that led into a small apartment fitted up as a morning-room or study. These details are important in view of what follows.

Supper was ready, but we explored the rest of the cottage before sitting down to it. I don't think we met with one disappointment. There was even a bathroom. 'So,' Tom said to me triumphantly, 'you won't have to sponge yourself over, standing up on one leg in a kind of degraded frying pan.'

Mrs Forran had arranged for a woman to come in every morning and do the rough work, since there was no room there for a servant to sleep. The woman was present when we arrived, and had prepared a hot meal for us. Her younger sister had come, too, to keep her company.

This Mrs Lubbock was a stumpy, silent creature, seemingly very nervous and stupid, and it was hard to get more than a word out of her. She did not know to whom the cottage belonged, or so she said. A gentleman named Sellinger used to come and stop there, but him she had hardly seen, and knew nothing about. She looked nervously around her as she said this, and left as soon as we would let her, dragging her sister with her.

In the interval between her departure and our sitting down to the roast ham and fowls, Tom nodded to me to come into the kitchen. I did so, and he pointed to the inside of the door, on which a cross had been roughly drawn with a piece of white chalk. I looked at him and saw him smiling, his eyebrows lifted.

'That's that woman,' he remarked. 'Do you know what it means, Archie?'

'I suppose it means that she thinks the house is haunted,' I said, 'I should think the people round here are pretty superstitious. They generally are in these lonely places.'

Tom sank his voice.

'Don't say anything to Jack,' he whispered.

'Pooh! Jack doesn't believe in spooks. He's not such a fool.'

'Nevertheless, he's not himself these days, and we won't take any risks. Look out!'

He took out his handkerchief and smudged the chalk marks until the cross was obliterated.

'By Jove,' he added, 'this is "some" cottage! Ghost and all!'

'We ought to have a sweepstake,' I suggested. 'The money to go to the first who sees it.'

'Could we trust each other, do you think?' said Tom, and we both laughed.

It would be well to explain at once that none of us believed in what is commonly called the supernatural. We were normal, hard-headed people, even more sceptical concerning such things as ghosts than the average man in the street. At ordinary times we should have welcomed a ghost story connected with our dwelling-place, but, as Tom had said, Jack Forran was not quite himself.

During supper we criticised the cottage, and Jack was the only one who had something to say about it that fell short of praise.

'It's a ripping old place,' he said; 'but do you know it seems to me rather self-conscious of being a cottage.'

'What do you mean?' Mrs Forran laughed.

'I mean that everything about it—the furniture and all that—is so very "cottagey". It seems to keep on shouting at you: "I am a cottage. Everything in me is just right for a cottage." I don't express myself very well.'

Helen laughed.

'I know,' she said. 'You mean this room is, somehow, just a little stagey.'

'Stagey was just the very word I was trying to think of,' Jack said. Tom, who was sitting opposite Helen and me, looked around him. 'Do you know,' he said, 'that this room is just like a scene on the stage. Try and imagine that wall over there—the fourth wall I think it's called—has been taken down. On the floor is a row of footlights. Beyond it's all dark, and there is row after row of blurred faces.'

Mrs Forran nodded, and we all looked round at the fourth wall.

'Yes, I can imagine all that,' she said.

'Well, then,' Tom continued, 'Imagine yourself among the audience for a moment. You'd be looking on to the stage at a conventional stage cottage sitting-room. That door leading to the little room would be the exit on the prompt side. There's no exit on the other side, but the space behind the chimney looks like one. Open hearth on right. Two doors at back, grandfather's clock, oak beams, everything complete.'

We all marvelled, because it was in very truth a perfect stage cottage, and I immediately experienced what I took to be the power of suggestion. I was sitting beside Helen, with my back to the fourth wall, and I felt that there was no wall there. Behind me was a row of bright footlights, and a sea of dim faces. I could feel hundreds of eyes upon me, and even suffered for the moment a mild kind of stage fright.

Now I am not one given to nerves, nor is my imagination in the ordinary way a particularly active one. But on that occasion it seemed to slip out of my control, and I imagined not only that the fourth wall was down, but that all our little party began to behave in a certain precise and self-conscious manner as if they were acting before an audience. And I, too, although I strove against it, became one of the mummers.

When we spoke we pitched our voices in a slightly higher key, and made our articulation clearer. We addressed each other not in our usual manner, but as rather stiff strangers who had been placed at the same table at an hotel. Our table manners lost their freedom. Jack, who was inclined to sprawl in his chair, sat up straight as a ramrod. Tom, who had a habit of playing with his breadcrumbs while he was not actually eating, sat between the courses with his hands under the table. The idea that the wall was down and the audience watching our every movement and listening to every word seemed to have worked ridiculously on the minds of us all.

We were talking primly in our stupid stage voices about something quite unimportant, when Tom, who had been silent for a while, suddenly startled us. He raised his voice, and, looking over the heads of Helen and me, declaimed as follows:

'When I do fall in love, Heaven help me—and her!'

The voice was hardly his own; it was the sonorous, flexible voice of an actor. The words boomed from his lips, full of passion and sadness. I felt Helen start beside me. We had not been talking of love, and in the circumstances I had never heard a less pertinent speech. There was dead silence for nearly half a minute.

Then I felt a change come over me, as if a shadow had passed on from my mind. I felt no more the footlights behind me and the rows of faces, and suddenly set up a roar of laughter. Simultaneously all the others laughed.

Once again we were old friends, supping privately and behaving naturally, no longer mummers on a stage. We laughed until the tears ran down our cheeks.

'Oh, Tom, you idiot!' Helen cried.

'What on earth made you say that?' Mrs Forran demanded, choking.

Tom regarded us all, smiling but slightly flushed.

'I don't know,' he said. 'It must have sounded frightfully mad. The words came into my head, and I just said them.'

Afterwards they became a catch-phrase with us. Now we all repeated them, imitating Tom's voice, until Mrs Forran sniffed audibly, and looked towards the fire.

'Can you smell anything burning?' she asked.

We all could. There was a heavy smell of smoke in the air. It was as if a part of the carpet were smouldering.

'A spark must have jumped out of the fire,' I said; and went to see. But I could find nothing, although I searched the room, and presently the smell of burning went. We agreed that it was rather curious.

We had been at the cottage more than a week when, just after tea on a dark, drizzling evening, Tom begged me to come out for a walk with him. It was not inviting outside, and I was never glad to leave Helen, but the look in her brother's eyes made me aware that he had something to say to me. So I assented rather grudgingly, and put on my cap and Ulster.

Up to then we had had a good time. I was always happy when I was near Helen; Jack was already much better, and everybody was delighted at the signs he displayed of an early recovery. Moreover, we had had plenty of sport with our guns, and Jack had landed an eleven-pound pike on a spinner,

All that marred our pleasure was that sensation of being on the stage, to which all of us had to confess. Generally it came on at supper, and then we made frantic efforts to behave like our normal selves. Fifty times a day we bullied Tom for giving voice to the suggestion, and thus affecting all of us.

There was also a mystery, which we had given up trying to solve. Regularly every evening at about the same time we smelt something burning, and always we searched for a smouldering splinter on the carpet, and never found it. Jack had a theory beginning, 'When the wind is in a certain quarter . . .' which we accepted, but only because a poor explanation is better than none to people who do not care for being mystified.

As Tom and I picked our way down the dark garden, sucking at our pipes, I knew instinctively that he wanted to talk to me about the cottage. For some reason I did not care to be too serious, and as we reached the road I imitated his voice, saying:

'When I do fall in love, Heaven help me—and her!'

He laughed, but not very mirthfully.

'Yes,' he said, 'that was dashed queer. Archie, my dear lad, there are a lot of things that are very queer. Have you any vices?'

'Such as?'

'Going downstairs at night and reading your immortal short stories aloud to yourself?'

'Me!' I exclaimed. 'Good Lord, no! Why?'

'Well, Jack had a jolly good night's sleep last night, so it wasn't he. It certainly wasn't I. And now you say it wasn't you. And it was a man's voice.'

I felt an uncomfortable, prickly feeling in my skin.

'What are you talking about?' I asked.

He hesitated a moment.

'Look here,' he said, 'Helen's had a fright. You know her room is over the dining-room? Well, it seems she woke up last night quite late, and heard a man's voice in the room underneath. It sounded quite plain—so plain that she could almost hear the words. It was like somebody reading aloud with a lot of expression. She didn't know the voice.'

Again I felt that prickly sensation in my skin.

'She must have been dreaming,' I said.

My dear chap, a week ago I should have declared unhesitatingly that she was dreaming. But now I'm not so sure.'

'You say it was like somebody reading aloud?'

'Yes, with a lot of expression. An actor going through his part, for instance.'

He said this with an elaborate casualness, but I caught another note in his voice.

'Tom,' I said, 'don't be an idiot.'

He was silent for a short while. Presently he said:

'You don't believe in ghosts, of course?'

'No, I don't.'

'Nor did I until the last few days. It's no use howling me down, Archie, but there is something queer about that cottage. For instance, that sensation of being on the stage before an audience. We all get it at times. And the smell of burning. And the queer thing I said almost unconsciously that you all rag me about.'

I was already more than half convinced, but I tried to argue on the side of what I thought was sanity.

'Are you sure we haven't all caught nerves from poor old Jack?' I suggested.

'Nerves! Rubbish! Besides, old Jack is, luckily, the least affected by these things of all of us. That's because he doesn't believe in uncanny things, and he doesn't know all that we know. Helen told nobody but me about the man she heard reading, simply because she wanted it kept from Jack. And he doesn't know about the cross we found on the kitchen door. If anything happens to give him a bad shock—well, you know what the result might be. I think we ought to try to get him away.'

Still I argued.

'The cross we found on the kitchen door proves that the silly old charwoman thought the cottage was haunted. And you know what country people are.'

Tom looked at me queerly.

'Look here, old chap,' he said, 'when we came here we didn't believe in such things. We all rather prided ourselves on being hard-headed. But now don't you think, after what has happened, that we might as well revise our views a little? Even if we would like to believe otherwise, don't for Heaven's sake let us shut our eyes to proofs. Supernatural or not, there is something confoundedly queer about the place we're living in. If Jack gets a bad shock it may send him mad. And poor Helen's frightened.'

Those two arguments were enough to make me see that we ought to leave the cottage. But the problem of how to get Jack to go was not easily solved. He was so thoroughly in love with his surroundings that no trivial objection would dislodge him, while to tell him the truth would simply defeat our own ends.

We talked this over for some time, but found no way out of the difficulty.

Then Helen began to occupy all my thoughts, and I insisted on our going back. She was safe enough with Jack and Mrs Forran, but I felt somehow that my place was near her. And Tom grabbed me by the shoulder with his long fingers, and let me know by a peculiar chuckle that he understood.

The evening of the twenty-second of December will live long in my memory, and with good reason. Let me try to tell what happened plainly and straightforwardly, without the omission of any important detail, and yet without exaggeration.

We had then occupied the cottage for about a fortnight, and since my walk in the rain with Tom—when he had confessed his sudden belief in 'ghosts'—nothing of importance had happened. We had experienced as usual the smell of burning, and the queer sensation of being on the stage, but Helen had heard no more voices, nor had there been any fresh phenomena.

After tea on that particular evening it was arranged that we should drive into St Ives and do some shopping; but I, seeing a Heaven-sent opportunity to do some of the work which I had neglected of late, elected to stay behind. I will not pretend that I was not nervous, but I will stoutly maintain, until the last day I live, that my nerves played no part in deluding me.

At first, when I was left alone and sat down to write, I felt 'jumpy' and uncomfortable. But a couple of pipes soothed me, and I soon lost myself in my work. After a while my pen began to scrape, paused, and went on scraping in the old familiar way. The old grandfather's clock said 'tock-tock, tock-tock', until I got so used to his voice that it seemed to become part of the silence.

Work passes the time as quickly as play, and when I paused to light another pipe and looked up at the clock, I found, to my surprise, that more than two hours had slipped away. It would not be very long before the others returned, so I went on with my work at once, and became absorbed in it for another half-hour.

Then quite suddenly I felt grow upon me that feeling of self-consciousness that I was beginning to know so well. I felt that hundreds of eyes were upon me, that hundreds of people were waiting to see what I would do next, and hear what I would say. I felt the cold air of fear in my nostrils, a dreadful sinking in the stomach, a prickly feeling in the skin.

'Nerves!' I told myself; but I dared not raise my eyes. I sat still, with my gaze bent down upon the uncompleted sentence, my pen shaking in my fingers. The grandfather's clock ticked on slowly, and I sat quite still, the slave of fear.

At last, and never so slowly and stealthily, I raised my eyes. They rested upon the door leading into the morning-room, which stood ajar. It was dark inside, but certain things were dimly visible, and those things were unfamiliar.

I saw the half of a step-ladder, the corner of what looked like a rough wooden shed, and a piece of rope dangling. My heart gave a great leap, and then seemed to stop beating.

'Oh, my God!' was the thought that leaped into my brain. 'The wings of a theatre!'

I moved my gaze round a little to the left, and instead of seeing the wall—the fourth wall—I saw a space of semi-gloom. Beyond the carpet was a short space of bare boards, and then a row of footlights throwing up a yellow glare. In the gloom I saw faces, row upon row of them, the curves of a dress circle and gallery with a glint of light on their brass railings, and high up in a kind of dome a cluster of small lamps was burning dimly.

I sprang up with a little cry, and stood facing the ghastly change that had overtaken the wall. There was not a sound, but I was horribly conscious of the undivided attention of hundreds upon hundreds of eyes and ears. And as I stood, dumb and quaking, my nostrils caught an acrid whiff of smoke.

Simultaneously I heard a sharp scream behind me. A hoarse voice shouted something inaudible. Heavy footfalls began to ring on hollow boarding; I heard a hiss like an escape of steam, and the clatter of pails.

Then I spoke, and the voice sounded in no way like my own.

I said: 'If I do fall in love, Heaven help me—and her!'

I uttered the words without realising their meaning, and because I was powerless to do otherwise.

Then the faces of that ghastly audience dimmed, and finally vanished, cut off from me by a curtain of black smoke. The smoke was all around me in reeking clouds. It got into my eyes and my throat, and I fell forward, choking and gasping, on to my knees. An agony of suffocation tore me. As consciousness slipped away from me I have a dim memory of a great tongue of flame flickering a yard in front of my eyes . . .

It was Helen who found me lying on the floor. She had run in a little in advance of the others, and the sight of me, lying thus, gave her the greatest fright of her experience. What she said to me before I came round I never learned until we became engaged, and that is neither here nor there. After a minute the others came in, and I have a dim memory of being given brandy and led up to bed.

Next day I lied painfully to my fellow members of the household, assuring them that I was only the victim of a heart attack, the first of my experience. But later in the morning Tom came and sat on the edge of my bed, fixing me with a pair of quizzical eyes.

'Better now?' he asked.

'Much.'

'Then you can tell me what happened. Heart attack be hanged. I've already prepared Jack for what I'm going to tell him. We're going to clear out of this at once. Will you tell your story first, or shall I tell mine?'

I looked at him in surprise.

'Has anything fresh happened?'

'I found out something yesterday,' he answered. 'The cottage is supposed to be haunted, although nobody seems to know precisely in what way. But I've found out all about the man who used to live here, and it seems to fit in rather well with what we've all experienced. Shall I tell you?'

'Yes, do!'

'Well, then. Yesterday evening, while the others were buying groceries, I went in to an inn at St Ives to get a bottle of whisky. There was a farmer chap in the bar, and I started talking to him, and told him where we were stopping. He pricked up his ears at once, and asked if we'd seen the ghost. I told him no, and asked him about it. He said that the cottage was supposed to be haunted by a man named Sellinger, who had lived in it off and on for years.'

'An actor?'

'Yes, an actor. It seems he used to use the place always when he was resting. He was quite a celebrity in his way, although he was hardly known to the London stage. For years he'd been touring the provinces with a play called The Heart of Annette, in which he played the lead. There was a scene in the play which depicted the interior of an old cottage, and from that scene he copied the arrangement of the room downstairs in every detail.'

'Ah!' I said, and shuddered. Already I had a dim idea of what was coming.

'He loved this place,' Tom resumed, 'and every weekend he could spare he came down here. All his vacations, too, were spent here. You can imagine him going through his parts in that room downstairs.'

I nodded grimly. My imagination needed very little stimulation.

'About a year ago,' Tom continued, 'he met his death on the stage. He was playing at a theatre in the Midlands, and was in the middle of his scene in the cottage sitting-room when the stage caught fire. He was suffocated by the smoke. He had just said, "If I fall in love, Heaven help me—and her!" when the smoke and flame rushed in upon him. Those were his last words. Why, what's the matter, Archie?'

There is a theory that when a man loves the place he lives in, it remains imbued with his personality long after he has left it. There is another theory to the effect that the spirit of a very strong personality (such as the actor Sellinger had doubtless been) can impress upon the minds of living people mental pictures of places and incidents which have figured prominently in his life, and can even make them experience the sense of a certain smell—as of burning, for instance. The spirit could, indeed, on rare occasions actually 'control' a person still in the flesh, and make him utter words quite involuntarily. As to that, let each think as he will.

But we were practical people, and we did not theorise overmuch. We simply left the cottage and went to Malvern. Anybody may have that cottage at a very modest rental, but we do not recommend it. There may not be such things as ghosts, but there are a lot of things, pleasant and unpleasant, which are beyond our ken.

In the Courtyard

I am not going to put a date on this story. It happened at one of those few white Christmastides, when for once the snow and ice on the Christmas cards was in keeping with the actual climatic conditions. I was at the time—as you shall judge for yourself in reading of my conduct—extremely young. And that, alas! was not quite yesterday.

On the evening of the twenty-third of December my luggage and I arrived at The George at Rompingdon, to spend Christmas at the fine old inn which lost two-thirds of its trade on the day after the last coach rumbled and bumped over the miles between York and London. The real name of the town is not Rompingdon, nor is The George the correct name of the inn; but those with a gift for reading between lines will have little difficulty in guessing the real name of the town and even of the old hostelry.

Now for a youngster of gregarious habits and innumerable friends to bury himself alone in an old inn at Christmas seems so unnatural as to demand immediate explanation; and the explanation is that I was very young, and there was a girl, and—well, this is another occasion for reading between the lines.

I had spent most of the preceding summer in Cornwall, and at the Fowey Hotel, Fowey, I had met Mrs Baymont and her daughter Eleanor, and there followed three of the jolliest weeks of my life. Eleanor was an indefatigable walker, and I, who hated walking for walking's sake, found myself tramping with her joyously along the coast road to Polperro and back—fourteen good Cornish miles—to Restormel Castle, Par, and Mevagissey, and other places within reach which seemed deserving of a visit. As Mrs Baymont seemed to encourage my intimacy with her daughter, and as I was able to pretend to myself that I stood a little higher in Eleanor's esteem than a mere holiday companion, I enjoyed every moment of those long days on that romantic coast.

When at last the Baymonts departed Mrs Baymont gave me their address—Huntsford Lodge, near Rompingdon—and said that I really must come and see them. If I were ever down that way and didn't call she would be highly offended. So the pain of parting was tempered a little by the reflection that it was probably not for ever.

Had I been older I daresay I should have taken Mrs Baymont at her word and planted myself on the doorstep of Huntsford Lodge, cheerily announcing myself with, 'Well, here I am!' or some such phrase indicative of resolution and cool cheek. But I was a shy youth in those days, and a general invitation which I wanted to accept was a thing of terror to me.

Off and on during the following months I corresponded with Eleanor, and sent respectful messages to her mother. I signed myself always as hers 'very sincerely'. After unpleasantly long intervals I received letters back from Eleanor which lacked the warmth of our summer companionship. She signed them 'yours sincerely' without the 'very'; and Mrs Baymont was for ever sending me her kind regards—for which I had no use—and neglecting to send me that direct invitation which would have brought me to her door as soon as I could pack a bag and board a train. Being able to look at the affair from only one angle, I did not see how difficult it was for her to offer more than a general invitation to a comparative stranger.

Hope deferred maketh the heart sick; and I was sick at heart during the whole long autumn. At Christmas time I could stand it no longer and took the train for Rompingdon, not with the intention of calling on the Baymonts, but hoping that one of them would notice my forlorn figure haunting the streets. I had an excuse for being in Rompingdon which, thin and unconvincing as it must have appeared to anybody else, seemed good enough to me.

So behold me on the night of the twenty-third in my lonely glory at The George: for the commercial travellers, who were the principal users of the house, were all home for

Christmas, and I was literally the only visitor. Having the choice of many bedrooms I selected one which overlooked the long cobbled yard; and when I went to bed that night I looked out upon a world of unsullied white, and great flakes were dancing past my window on a slant of the wind.

The George, together with many other hostelries, belonged to a syndicate and was controlled by a manager whom I found to be a good fellow, a gentleman and an ex-army officer. We were both of us adepts at the almost-lost art of brewing punch, and sat up late that night by the coffee-room fire, testing the efficacy of each other's recipes. The fire was well stoked and the fine long raftered room lit by candles. The light of these focussed upon the highly polished surfaces of solid and almost priceless furniture. That room could have held a hundred people, and we were the only two to sit there among the shadows.

'Business is rather slack with you,' I remarked suddenly. 'It isn't—in the bar,' he answered, 'and we shall have our hands full here tomorrow night.'

'Christmas Eve?'

'Dance,' he said laconically. 'Of course, you haven't been over the house yet. There's a room down below where we can dance a hundred couples.'

I could quite believe him. Seen from the High Street The George looks only of moderate size; but when you have passed under the arch leading into the courtyard you are astonished at the depth of the building as compared with its frontage. Around this courtyard stretches an oak gallery over the stables, coach-houses, and servants' quarters, now 'converted', but outwardly the same as ever. There was still the window of the coach-office on the corner, and to me the whole place was still redolent of the posting days. I had almost expected to see whistling ostlers leading out a change of horses, pretty servant maids in mob caps, red-faced coachmen with many capes to their coats. It was such an inn yard as Herbert Railton loved to draw.

'What sort of dance is it?' I asked. 'Subscription?'

He smiled at me.

'It is, and it isn't. That is to say that Tom, Dick, and Harry can't buy a ticket and walk in. My being a publican and a sinner excludes me. It's a county affair, and we're very exclusive hereabouts.'

'Not the County or Hunt Ball?' I exclaimed; for although these functions usually occurred near Christmas, I had never heard of one taking place on Christmas Eve.

'Oh, no. It's a fancy dress dance in aid of the County Hospital. Tickets two guineas. Three or four of our local bigwigs are running it and tickets are only obtainable through them. If you've any friends in the neighbourhood you could get in, of course. Were you thinking of going?'

'I've only just heard about it for the first time,' I said. And then, seeing that he was a little puzzled at my having come to stay there at such a time, I brought out the excuse which was to serve me when I met the Baymonts.

'You see,' I added, i don't know this part of the world at all. I'm writing a book called Old English Coaching Inns, and I heard that this was one which had to be visited.'

He seemed pleased, as indeed he ought to have been.

'That will mean,' he said, 'an extra crop of American visitors next summer. You'll let me know when the book's coming out and where I can get a copy? Well, I doubt if there's a finer inn of this type in the country. It's a place with a history, too. Cromwell, Pepys, Marlborough—not to mention Dick Turpin on his way to York—have all stopped here. I'll point out the Turpin room tomorrow when I show you over. He seems to have stopped at every inn along the road on his mythical ride to York, but you needn't mention that in your history.'

I promised that I would not.

'You ought to have a ghost here,' I added, half in fun. 'Have you?'

He reached down for the poker and broke a great knob of coal on the fire, making the flames mount to the edge of the chimney.

'I don't know,' he said, 'that a ghost is always a good advertisement.'

'There is one, then?' said I.

'There's supposed to be one. There's supposed to be one in nearly every old house, isn't there? Not that this one is in the house . . .'

He paused and I waited, but he had come to a stop.

'What is the story?' I asked.

'I don't know it,' he answered. 'I only know that there is one. But as nobody ever sees the ghost it's hardly worth troubling about. I daresay you'll find a few old people about the town who know the legend if you wish to hear it.'

I could see his point. His directors might object to a ghost story being published, as likely to frighten away customers. While I thought this was absurd I could sympathise with him for not wishing to shoulder the responsibility of telling me the tale. After all he was only the manager.

Next morning after breakfast he showed me all over the wonderful old house, and afterwards I sallied forth to take a look at the old town, which, with snow upon its roofs and pavements, looked sleepier than ever. I was coming out of a tobacconist's when the sound of a fast-trotting horse upon the road made me look up; and then it seemed to me that my heart stopped beating. Approaching me along the High Street was a light dog cart drawn by a high-stepping grey, with a groom perched behind upon the tailboard, and—Eleanor was driving it!

I had come to Rompingdon especially to see her, but now that we were face to face my courage nearly failed me. On the instant I saw the thinness of my excuse for having come to Rompingdon. It was so obviously for the purpose of seeing her that I had had the insolence and the effrontery to make the journey! Almost I was tempted to make a bolt for it, but Eleanor saw me and the reins in her hands tightened. It would be hard to say which of us coloured the more vividly. Ah me! I think I mentioned that this was not quite yesterday!

Somehow the dog cart came to the edge of the pavement and I found myself standing hat in hand looking up at Eleanor. The groom, meanwhile, had jumped down and gone to the horse's head, and seemed to be studying the weather-vane on the spire of the parish church.

I don't remember what we said to each other at first. I only know that I began to blurt out my excuse for being there with a glib rapidity which must have been the final disproof of its truth. She would not say that she herself was glad to see me. The best I could get from her was:

'Mother will be so surprised and pleased to hear you have come down.'

Precious time was passing and still no invitation to Huntsford Lodge. I began to wonder how long it would be considered seemly for me to hold her there in conversation while the horse was catching cold, when at last she tossed me a crumb.

'Oh,' said she, as if on an inspiration, 'you must come to the Hospital Dance tonight. It's at The George, where you are staying. Mother and I will be there. I want two guineas from you.'

It was in the days of golden sovereigns. Gladly I produced two of them and a florin.

'I'll have your ticket sent round to you,' she said. 'Fancy dress, please.'

Despair struck at me again.

'Where on earth can I get a fancy dress in this one-eyed hole?' I wanted to know.

'Don't call our county town a one-eyed hole, please. Can't you go as a pierrot?'

'I could easily—if I had the clothes.'

She seemed to consider, 'It's such an easy costume. It's a pity the time is so short. I know. Jump up here!'

I needed no second bidding. In a trice I was beside her.

'All right, George,' she said to the groom.

Half a minute later we were on the move, and I was as happy as a saint on his way to heaven. So happy was I, indeed, that a minute or two elapsed before it occurred to me to ask where we were going. Then Eleanor began to laugh; I could feel her beside me shaking deliciously.

'There's a nice little woman, a dressmaker, who lives in Newmarket Road. I give her a job occasionally. A pierrot costume's so easy to make. I'm sure she could do it for you in time.'

I was jealous of my dignity in those days, and I could almost feel the amusement of the man sitting behind us. But I joined in her merriment, for I could not help being glad. At least it showed that she wanted me to come to the dance.

Eleanor drew up before a small villa with a brass plate on the gate, and we presently interviewed a grey-haired woman who wore glasses and an air of business.

'This gentleman,' said Eleanor, 'is Mr Maurice Gage. He wants to come to the dance tonight, but hasn't a fancy dress. Do you think you could make him anything in time? A pierrot costume?'

The dressmaker said that she would do her best. Her work-people were all extremely busy.

'Promise!' I begged. 'Promise I can have it by eight o'clock.'

Reluctantly she promised. Eleanor waved her hand to me and made for the door.

'Bye-bye, Maurice,' she said. 'See you tonight. If you don't come'

She left the threat unfinished and fluttered away, leaving me to the tender mercies of the dressmaker, who took some superficial measurements.

'How much are you going to charge me?' I asked when she had done.

She named a figure which seemed to me absurdly low.

'I'll pay double,' I said, 'if I get the clothes in time.'

At eight o'clock I dined hastily in morning dress and then went round to the hotel office to see if any parcel had come for me. None had. It was then half-past, and the wretched dressmaker had broken faith. Poor woman, I ought to have been sorry for her, but I was utterly selfish.

I then went into the bar and drank a whisky and soda in the company of some jolly townspeople who were all wishing each other a merry Christmas. They came in white with snow, for it was a terrible night outside; and one old fellow with a bottle in each side pocket of his overcoat and a turkey under his arm might have stepped straight out of a Christmas number plate. But I was too anxious about my costume to feel the true spirit of Christmas. If it did not come I felt that I could not go. I was not going to appear ridiculous by being the only man present in evening dress. Once again I must remark that I was very young in those days.

After a while I went once more to the office, and found old Charles the waiter in the vestibule. Nothing had yet come for me, and I told Charles my trouble. He was doubly sympathetic in expectation of a Christmas box.

'Directly it comes, sir,' he said, I'll let you know, never fear.'

So I went back to the bar and stayed there until the wail of violins from the ballroom drove me nearly frantic. Restlessness drove me to my bedroom, where, by looking out of my window, I could see the lights of the ballroom piercing the chinks of the blind and lying in dazzling bars across the snow in the courtyard.

I have already mentioned that my window overlooked this yard. The ballroom, I ought to explain, was a long room on the ground floor running nearly the length of the yard. It had once been several rooms, but the partition walls had been taken down to make way for three full-sized billiard tables which were never purchased; so that it became instead a place for dances and public dinners. I could hear the music quite plainly. Behind those lighted blinds Eleanor—my Eleanor—was swinging to the strains of the 'Blue Danube' with another man's arm about her waist. And all through that infernal dressmaker.

I had not yet given up all hope. I turned away from the window and took off my collar and tie in order to change the quicker if, or when, my parcel arrived. Then I went back to the window again and looked out. An instant later my face was pressed to the pane and my breath had frosted it. An exclamation broke from my lips.

'Silly asses!' I exclaimed to myself. 'They'll catch their deaths of cold and spoil their clothes.'

There were three people in the courtyard—three people who had evidently strayed from the ballroom, for they were dressed in the fashion of the middle eighteenth century. I could see the two men and the girl quite plainly in the light which escaped from the ballroom windows.

The two men were skylarking. Swords formed a part of their eighteenth century costume, and they had dragged these from their scabbards and were fighting as pretty a duel as you could wish to see. They knew something of swordsmanship too, and while I thought them fools for fooling in the snow, I could admire the play they made with those long rapiers which flashed out dazzlingly whenever they crossed a bar of light.

At first I could see the faces of none. Then the girl raised her eyes and looked up towards my window, and I was amazed to see that it was Eleanor. What part was she playing, I wondered, in this idiotic charade? For some sort of charade I deemed it to be, because her eyes and features simulated great horror and fear. I waved to her, but she took no notice.

Suddenly one of the combatants lifted his sword and received the point of his adversary's weapon—always a blunt point to these fancy-dress swords—clean over the heart. The fellow, I judged, was a good actor. There was nothing of the conventional stage fall in the way he came down. He dropped like a dead man, bending simultaneously at the knees, waist, and neck, and sinking into a heap. An excellent bit of acting, but why on earth . . .

There came a sudden knock on my door behind me, and I looked round.

Charles the waiter was in the room, holding aloft in triumph a fat parcel.

'It's just come, sir. I looked for you in the bar and in the coffee-room and then tried here. The lady that brought it says she's sorry she's a bit late, but she did her best.'

'That's fine,' I exclaimed, crossing the room and taking it from his hand. 'Now I can get on with the good work. They seem to be having a good time at the dance.'

'A very good time I should say, sir.'

'Two of 'em are out in the yard now, pretending to fight a duel.'

I saw Charles's jaw suddenly drop, for all the world as if I hadn't said 'pretending'.

'Oh,' I exclaimed lightly, 'it's only play,' and went once more to the window. To my astonishment the yard was empty, save for the drifting snow and the light from the ballroom windows.

'They've gone in now,' said I. 'Don't blame them either. Why, what's the matter, Charles?'

The old waiter's face was grey. He reached out a shaking hand and clutched the back of a chair.

'Beg pardon, sir, was there a lady with them?'

'Yes. Why, you must have seen them yourself.'

'No, I 'aven't seen 'em—I 'aven't seen 'em—thank God!' The old waiter's manner disturbed and alarmed me.

'Charles,' I exclaimed, 'for goodness' sake what's the matter with you?'

'Nothing, sir. I beg pardon. These stairs. I'm not as young as I was, and my 'eart's a bit weak. If you'll excuse me, sir, I'll go down and get myself a drop o' brandy.'

He went, leaving me puzzled. I was still more puzzled half an hour later. On arriving in the ballroom I had the tact to seek out Mrs Baymont first of all. I found her in an alcove among the chaperones and the card tables. She addressed me as Maurice, as she had begun to do at Fowey, and there was a little twinkle in her eyes for which I was grateful if the least bit embarrassed.

'So you've come down at last,' she said. 'So glad to see you, Maurice. What a long time it seems since the summer, doesn't it?'

There was a stout dowager, grey-haired and of sentimental aspect sitting beside her—a Lady Hillyer. Mrs Baymont presented me, and then began to talk mischievously of me to her.

'Mr Gage has come down here to write a book about Coaching Inns. Imagine it—at Christmas time! Such devotion—to one's work! We met him down in Cornwall, you know. You were not working very hard then, were you, Maurice? Do you know, Gladys, he's treated us most shamefully?' The dowager's lips curved with amusement; her eyes were bright with sentimental emotion. I could have killed her without the least grain of remorse.

'I told him,' Mrs Baymont continued, 'to come down and see us whenever he felt inclined. It's taken him six months to get here, and now he's here he stays at The George, if you please, and has only come at all to write about the inn. What do you think of him, Gladys?'

I didn't listen to what she thought of me. I was blushing all over, 'It's a pity you're so busy,' went on Mrs Baymont, who half a century before would undoubtedly have been called a 'quizz'. i want to ask him over for the day tomorrow, Gladys, but I hardly like to risk a rebuff. He'll probably tell us that he's working—even on Christmas Day.'

Then, seeing she had teased me enough, she plucked at the black pom-pom on the sleeve of my pierrot's tunic.

'There, there, Maurice,' she said kindly, 'run away and dance with the girls. And come over to us tomorrow. I'll send the carriage for you after breakfast and you shall take us to church.'

I made good my escape without having told Mrs Baymont that I had seen Eleanor out in the snow watching a mock duel. It was no part of my policy to get Eleanor scolded for risking a severe cold. And when I found Eleanor I had the shock of my life.

Half an hour before I had seen her out in the snow dressed like a lady of the eighteenth century. But I found myself bowing to the jolliest Dutch girl who had never set foot in Holland. Her programme was not quite full—although I dared not hope that she had saved dances for me—but it was by the time I had done with it. I stumbled through a polka with her for about a minute, and then took her to sit down and talk in the small room next to the buffet.

'Extravagance,' I said to her, 'is—or ought to be—one of the Seven Deadly Sins. I've never before heard of a girl wearing two costumes at the same dance.'

'I've never heard of it yet!' said Eleanor.

I regarded her more in sorrow than in anger.

'Really!' I exclaimed in mock disdain. 'Considering I saw you not three-quarters of an hour ago wearing a sort of eighteenth century thing-me-bob. I was watching from my window, and I saw you out in the snow watching two silly asses pretend to fight a duel. You're going to get the dickens of a chill for that. After this hot room it's enough'

I broke off, finding her staring at me in the sort of manner which bereft me of speech. It was as if I had made some dreadful faux pas in speaking of the matter. Vaguely I remembered the effect of my words on poor old Charles the waiter.

'Maurice,' she exclaimed, 'are you joking?'

'Where's the joke?' I inquired, I'm only saying that I saw'

'I know! I know! Maurice, will you swear that you saw me?'

'Certainly. But I don't see why. Why, what's the matter, Eleanor?'

Her head had fallen back a little and she began to ply her fan gently to and fro.

'I think I should like . . . yes, would you mind getting me ... a little champagne cup? It's dreadfully hot in here.'

I went and got it for her. Charles, on hearing of the goings-on outside, had fled to the brandy bottle. Eleanor had had recourse to that lighter beverage which young women may be seen sipping in public. Quite permissibly, I think, I was puzzled and bewildered.

When I returned to her she said:

'You won't say a word to mother—about that?'

'Of course not, since you ask me,' I answered.

I arrived at Huntsford Lodge next morning in time to join the party of half-a-dozen that set out for the village church. By the evening we were twenty strong, a contingent having arrived for dinner, dancing, and games. After dinner, when we men left the dining-room, we found the ladies clustered around the fire in the hall nibbling chocolates and preserved fruit, and pulling crackers alleged to contain jewellery, but which shed nothing more exciting than coloured paper caps. We joined the group, waiting for somebody to suggest something to do, and each of us secretly hoping that that 'something' would not be too violent.

Somebody suggested that ghost stories should be told, and somebody else lowered the lights. I did not mind this, for I had stationed myself beside Eleanor, although I had hitherto noticed that viva voce ghost stories are generally dull and lacking in the authentic thrill.

I was the sixth to perform. The previous five told stories alleged to be true, which I had either read as frank fiction or of which I had heard variations since I was a child of ten. My turn came, and I told of the experience of a friend of mine, and conveniently forgot to mention that he was the most notorious liar I knew. It was Mrs Baymont who concluded that part of the evening's entertainment, and in a manner which I shall never forget.

'Isn't there a ghost here?' somebody asked her.

'Not that we know of.'

'But I thought there was a family ghost,' somebody else demurred.

'So there is. It—or rather they—belong to my late husband's family, but they're not seen here. It's down at The George'

Eleanor's voice broke in, nervously and with a sort of childish petulance.

'Oh, not that story, mother!'

'Why not? Don't be so foolish, Eleanor. If anybody who hasn't heard it cares to hear it . . .'

A chorus of voices interrupted, expressing a desire to hear it. I heard Eleanor beside me give vent to a little round 'Oh!' of remonstrance below her breath. You may imagine how I pricked up my ears: first, because Eleanor did not want the story to be told, and secondly, because the manager of The George had hinted at such a tale. Mrs Baymont folded her hands in her lap and settled herself to tell it.

'This ghost story,' she said, 'belongs to my late husband's family, or rather to the Motterys, from whom he was descended on the distaff side. Until ten years ago the Motterys lived out here at Leake Hall, not twenty miles away; and, properly speaking, the story belongs to them.

'Now about a hundred and fifty years ago Sir George Mottery—the heads of that house were all Georges and Jameses—had a beautiful daughter named Barbara, from whom Eleanor is descended; for she married Lionel Baymont, my husband's great-great—several greats—grandfather. I am afraid, though, that she was forced into her marriage with him, as this story may show.

'Sir George Mottery was a heavy-drinking man of violent passion; Barbara was obstinate and high-spirited; the two tugged in opposite directions, as it were. She fell in love with a neighbouring squire, a presentable boy of good yeoman stock, and by no means a pauper; so that nowadays one can hardly understand why he wasn't considered good enough for the Motterys. Anyhow, Sir George would have none of him, so the young couple tried to solve the problem by eloping.

'Now this road—the Great North Road—takes one to Gretna sooner or later, so it was the way of nearly all runaway couples from this part of the country. The young people were successful in getting away, and posted safely into Rompingdon, but either Sir George was on the watch or part of their plans miscarried, for, unknown to them, the indignant father was hot on their heels. While their horses were being changed, he surprised them in the yard of the inn.'

I was never a man greatly susceptible to shocks, but I must admit feeling a prickly sensation under my skin. Already I knew what was coming.

'Sir George pulled out his sword and there and then attacked the boy, who had to pull out his own weapon and defend himself. The poor distracted girl had to stand by and watch a duel to the death between her father and her lover; and I don't suppose she knew herself which of them she wanted to win. Now the story goes that the boy was immeasurably the better swordsman, and had her father at his mercy all the while, but could not bring himself to wound or kill Sir George in her presence. Tiring at last, he lifted the point of his sword, and Sir George ran him through the heart, killing him at Barbara's feet.'

I still felt that prickly sensation under my skin, and I looked at Eleanor, but I could not get her to look at me.

'Now,' continued Mrs Baymont, 'the story goes that on snowy nights the departed spirits of those three come back to re-enact that tragic scene in the yard of The George. But—they are only to be seen by descendants of the poor girl, or to those bound to one of her descendants by ties of love and devotion. So none of you need be afraid of seeing them.'

Dimly I heard laughing protests on all sides. Everybody assured Mrs Baymont and Eleanor of his, or her, love and devotion. I—well, I felt that the three poor ghosts had done me a good turn by proving mine.

'But nobody's ever really seen them,' said the inevitable Sadducee.

'I know of two who think they did. My late husband's old nurse swore that she peeped into the yard one snowy night and saw two men in strange clothes fighting a duel with swords and a girl watching them in an agony of despair. And my husband himself died convinced that he had seen the same thing. It was about ten years ago, and he was taking the chair at a dinner given to the Conservative candidate in the very room where we were dancing last night. After the dinner and the speeches he went to one of the windows and looked out to see if the snow had stopped. And quite plainly he saw the three figures, the two men fighting and the young girl with despair and terror on her face. Eleanor was only ten at the time, but he noticed how alike she was in features to the—well, it must have been the ghost of Barbara, I suppose. And that is rather curious, for Eleanor is, of course, a direct descendant.'

People had listened all the while with the usual polite incredulity. Most of them, I am sure, were privately thinking that the dinner to the Conservative candidate must have been a good dinner, to which the late Mr Baymont had done more than justice. That story was the last of the ghostly tales. I was glad, because others would have seemed weak as water to me after that. Besides, I had something to say to Eleanor. Up went the lights. Somebody took possession of the drawing-room piano, leaving open the door of the room, and in a few minutes informal dancing had begun.

Eleanor pointedly avoided me, dancing with two other men before I could comer her. I went round with her once in silence, and then led her protesting and almost struggling into the empty dining-room.

'Oh, what is it? What is it?' she cried out sharply, petulantly.

I let go of her and faced her.

'Well?' I said.

'Well?' she answered; and then, 'Do you still think you saw me out in the snow last night?'

'Do you mean to say,' I exclaimed, 'that I've seen a ghost?'

'I think,' she answered, 'that you've seen three. But—don't tell people. Don't tell anybody. They won't believe you. And—I don't want them to think that you—that you'

She broke the sentence off short and little voices inside me seemed to sing because she cared what people thought about me. But I was still amazed. Until that evening I'm not sure that I had ever really believed in ghosts.

'I'm very glad your mater told that story,' I said, I'm not a member of the family, so—so it proves something, doesn't it? Don't you see, Eleanor? "Ties of love and devotion"'

She was suddenly all pale and trembling.

'Love and devotion,' she repeated in a voice all low and shaken. 'And you haven't been near us all these months. And you wouldn't have come near us if I hadn't met you in the street'

'Eleanor!' I exclaimed, taking a step towards her. if you only knew how afraid I was to come. Love and devotion. There it is—proved. You can't deny it, Eleanor!'

I had taken her hands before she looked up at me, and then my heart leaped up at what I saw—the sudden soft light in her eyes, the beauty of them, and their dawning wonder.

'After all,' she murmured with only the least spice of mischief, 'you've come a long way, haven't you—to write about The George? And at Christmas, too!'

We were standing by the door, which stood ajar. With great presence of mind, although perhaps a little clumsily, I closed it with my elbow as I took her into my arms.

A.M. Burrage – The Life And Times.

Alfred McLelland Burrage, better known as simply AM Burrage, was born in Hillingdon, Middlesex on July 1st, 1889, to Alfred Sherrington Burrage and Mary E. Burrage. On his Father's side writing already ran in the family's blood as both he and an uncle, Edwin Harcourt Burrage, were writers of the then very popular boys' magazine fiction.

Life in late Victorian times was by no means easy and writing has always been a precarious career for most. For an insight into the young AM and his surroundings it is interesting to see how certain facts were captured in the 1891 census when he was aged one. The family is listed as living at Uxbridge Common in Hillingdon. His father is 40 and his mother 36. In the next census of 1901, and with it the end of the Victorian era, the family has moved to 1 Park Villa, Newbury. In that time his father has aged 17 years his mother 6 years and young AM has disappeared from the records. It's almost a precursor to one of his stories.

There is little documented about his growing up and education. What we can glean though is something about his environment. His neighbours were varied: a tailor's journeyman, a corn porter, a lodging-house keeper and a grocer's assistant. Nothing particularly illustrious, so times cannot have been as rosy as they should, especially in the light of his Father's hard work. Alfred Sherrington wrote for The Boy's World, Our Boys' Paper, The Boys of England, and various others. He also appears to have written under the pseudonym Philander Jackson and edited The Boys' Standard and that one of his more celebrated pieces was a retelling of the story of Sweeney Todd entitled "The String of Peals; or, Passages from the Life of Sweeney Todd, the Demon Barber".

Sadly Alfred Sherrington Burrage died in 1906. There is a biographical note in Lloyd's Magazine, from 1921, which suggests that young Alfred McLelland was studying at St. Augustine's, the Catholic Foundation School in Ramsgate, and most probably away from home at the time.

A.M. Burrage was 16 years old when he had his first story published; the same year as his father's death, in the prestigious boys' paper, Chums. It was a great start to his professional career and whether doors had been opened by his father and family or not the young man's career now had to stand on its own. He was now primary provider for the household and this was the only way he could do it. His Mother, sister and aunt must be provided for.

Magazine fiction was his family's blood and business and for A. M. Burrage, business was good. He established himself as a competent and creative writer and was busy writing stories and articles on a weekly basis for publications such as Boys' Friend Weekly, Boys' Herald, Comic Life, Vanguard, Dreadnought, Triumph Library Cheer Boys Cheer, and Gem, under the pseudonym 'Cooee'.

However, unlike his father and uncle who had remained firmly and easily categorised as boys' writers, he had his sights set on the more well regarded, more lucrative, adult market. Burrage was aided in his early years as a professional writer by Isobel Thorne of the off-Fleet Street publishing firm Shurey's. Her publications have been characterised as "low in price, modest in payments, but whose readers were avid for romance, thrills, sensation, strong characterisation and neat plotting", and this estimation of her publications also fits nicely the description of Burrage's own writing at that time. For a young writer this sort of readership was vital, and the modest wages he received were bolstered by the exposure the publications brought him. Burrage was certainly helped by Thorne's use of young writers.

At the time Burrage was beginning to really establish himself as a writer, the entire magazine fiction scene was benefiting from what we would now see as disruptive influences: new printing techniques, a growing readership with more disposable income and leisure time and other media failing to provide – though obviously movies and such were only in their infancy at the time. The market was lively and commercial, and the readership interested, excitable and willing to pay. P. G. Wodehouse, of Jeeves fame, recalls these years:

We might get turned down by the Strand, but there was always the hope of landing with Nash's, the Story-teller, the London, the Royal, the Red, the Yellow, Cassell's, the New, the Novel, the Grand, the Pall Mall, and the Windsor, not to mention Blackwood's, Cornhill, Chambers's and probably about a dozen more I've forgotten.

With War clouds darkening the skies of Europe in 1914 Burrage was firmly established as a magazine writer, securing publication in London Magazine and The Storyteller, which were both highly prestigious publications. Alongside he had plenty printed in less illustrious publications such as Short Stories Illustrated.

By now Burrage, a young man of twenty-four-year-was eligible for the Armed Services. Under the 'Derby Scheme' he confirmed that he was available for service if called upon in December 1915. Conscription was to follow shortly though, by that time, Burrage had already voluntarily enrolled in the Artists Rifles.

The significance of Burrage's decision to join the Artists Rifles is made clear by the nature of the unit itself. They formed in the middle of the nineteenth century, a group of volunteer artists comprising musicians, writers, painters and engravers. Minerva and Mars were their patrons, one of wisdom, arts, and defence, the other of war. The unit boasted several significant figures as ex-servicemen, including Dante Gabriel Rossetti, Algernon Charles Swinburne and William Morris. It was a popular unit with students and recent postgraduates, and the training was considered and extensive.

In Burrage's vivid, celebrated account of World War I entitled War is War, he insists that he was a volunteer and not a conscript, though as has already been noted, it is quite possible that his decision to join such a respected territorial unit may have been more of an effort to secure himself a more congenial army posting; had he waited for conscription, he would have had little choice over those with whom he was posted. Unlike poets Wilfred Owen or Edward Thomas, Burrage did not achieve a commission, and he suggests in War is War that this may be a result of his extremely unmilitary personality and his shortcomings as a soldier.

Add to this the fact that as the breadwinner for the family he was putting himself in harm's way. If anything were to happen to him the result on the family would be devastating. With the death of
Edwin Harcourt Burrage in 1916 it came even more starkly into focus.

Even though he was now a soldier he was still a writer and writers had to write. It also helped that it was a distraction from the mindless carnage around him. He experimented with various genres, excelling in the one that was to prove most lucrative for him; the light romance, in which a male character invariably meets a female character, there is a problem or hurdle to their being together, they overcome it and they live happily ever after. Burrage's talent for this formula was such that he could work seemingly endless minor variations from the same basic storyline and so he was able to keep writing a steady body of easy work.

He gives a fascinating account of the practicalities of writing such fiction during wartime in War is War, in which he remarks on the difficulties of censorship: "the problem of censorship was an acute one to me. It was well enough to write a story, but the difficulty was to get it censored. Officers were shy of tackling five thousand words or so, written in indelible pencil..." After some time he managed to find a chaplain who was willing to undertake the censorship. However, in order to secure this chaplain's favour and thus his services he was obliged to appear to be holy. Though he did so in earnest while he was with the chaplain, his efforts were dashed when the chaplain found him, sprawled on top of a young girl, and realised Burrage's piety to be a fraudulent con. As Burrage had anticipated, the reality of his behaviour ensured that this particular opportunity was swiftly ended. Resourceful to the last, though, he writes of his solution: "there were 'green envelopes' which could be sent away sealed and were liable only to censorship at the base, but these were only sparingly issued... I met an A.S.C. lorry driver who had stolen enough green envelopes to last me for the rest of the war; and since he only wanted two francs for them I was free of the censorship from that day forward."

Although we know that Burrage had his family to support at home as an incentive to keep writing, at times in War is War he reveals a more intimate aspect of his relationship with his work.

"It was a great relief to me to write when it was at all possible – to sit down and lose myself in that pleasant old world I used to know and pretend to myself that there never had been a war. Some of my editors seemed of the opinion that we were not suffering from one now. One used to write to me saying "Couldn't you let me have one of your light, charming love stories of country house life by next Thursday." I would get these letters in the trenches during the usual 'morning hate' when my fingers were too numb to hold a pencil, when I was worn out with work and sleeplessness, and when I was extremely doubtful if there ever would be another Thursday".

Writing is a useful therapy and for Burrage it provided a means to escape if only for a short time to a world that he could control and move at will.   With the misery and harsh conditions of the War dragging on he was eventually invalided and so he returned to England.

One of the best insights we have as to the character which Burrage presented on his return from the war is to be found in Lloyd's's 1920 publication of Captain Dorry, one of Burrage's story series. In that publication there was included a brief sketch of Burrage, describing his personality.

A.M. BURRAGE is the type of young man who might very well walk out of one of his own stories. He commenced yarn-spinning as a boy of fifteen at St Augustine's, Ramsgate, writing stories of school life to provide himself with pocket-money. Since then he has won his spurs as one of the most popular of magazine writers. Everything he does has charm and reflects his own romantic spirit – for he is incurably romantic and hopelessly lazy. It is his misfortune, although he would not admit it, that his work finds a too ready market. Nevertheless, his friends hope that one day he will wake up and do justice to himself. Otherwise he may end up as a "best-seller", a fate which doubtless he contemplates with equanimity.

Despite the sketch's fairly accurate but negative summation of Burrage's literary output up to that point, some of his stories seem to exhibit a desire to write about more than just his usual romantic plots. The most immediate change of this nature is in his decision to bring some of his wartime experience into his work, despite being perfectly aware that such writing was not at all what his editors desired, for they feared it would upset and intimidate their readership.

An example of this can be found in "A Town of Memories", published in 1919 in Grand Magazine, in which he uses his well rehearsed romantic story with a slight shift of emphasis to explore his own return from the war and the general reception which soldiers received on their return. Following a young officer as he returns to the town in which he grew up, Burrage portrays an almost hostile environment into which he returns; he is unrecognised, and nobody pays any interest, respect or attention to him or his stories of the war, nor even to his reception of the Distinguished Service Order. Instead, the people of the town have their own interests and priorities with which to concern themselves. Though this contentious portrayal of post-war society certainly marks a slight shift in Burrage's writing, he returns to the romantic convention expected of him by reuniting the officer with a beautiful girl who had admired him throughout school. It would be harsh to not accept that market conditions expected one thing and to ignore them would mean turning his back on publications who still clamoured for his penmanship.

Another of Burrage's alternative directions is to be found in "The Recurring Tragedy", in which a General whose war tactics of attrition had been to the slaughtered cost of his soldiers, and he comes to re-imagine his own past as a Judas figure in a terrible vision. The Strange Career of Captain Dorry became a series for Lloyd's Magazine in 1920 about a gentleman crook and an ex-officer with a Military Cross who, idle in peacetime, meets a mysterious man called Fewgin whose business is in stolen goods and mind reading. Fewgin realises Dorry is a suitable candidate for recruitment into his gang of like-minded ex-military thieves, stealing only from "certain vampires who made money out of the war, and, by keeping up prices, are continuing to make money out of the peace". Again, in this motive, we see a glimpse of Burrage's own feelings on the war, as there is undoubtedly a bitterness towards those profiting from the suffering of others in such a manner. Fewgin justifies himself, saying:

"I help brave men who cannot help themselves. I give them a chance to get back a little of their own from the men who battened and fattened on them, who helped to starve their dependents while they were fighting, who smoked fat cigars in the haunts of their betters, and hoped the war might never end."

Burrage began to see slightly more success in the 1920s, achieving a couple of hard back publications entitled Some Ghost Stories and Poor Dear Esme. The latter, a comedy, concerns a boy who, for various reasons, is forced to disguise himself as a girl. Though these hard cover publications were a notable achievement, and one of which he was proud, the fact was that there was less money in it than in the magazines. In his history of the Strand Magazine, Reginald Pound portrays Burrage around this time, likening him to his equally prolific contemporary Herbert Shaw, considering them "two Bohemian temperaments that suffused and at times confused gifts from which more was expected than come forth. They had a precise knowledge of the popular short story as the product of calculated design. Both privately despised it, though it was their living."

The early 1920s, and with them a boom in prosperity, hope and happiness, now brought with them an increase in demand for war stories. Rather than preferring to ignore the atrocities of the war, which had seemed the general attitude in the immediate post-war years, society became more interested and concerned with the manner in which the war was fought, and the greed and political battles which had necessitated such bloodshed. Burrage answered this demand in 1930 with his own epochal piece, War Is War. He published under the pseudonym 'Ex-Private X', saying "were it otherwise I could not tell the truth about myself", though its publisher, Victor Gollancz, "who published the book and greatly admired it, had to point out that the critics would hardly take the book seriously if it became known that the author earned his living producing two or three slushy love stories a week".

In one of a series of letters he wrote to his contemporary and fellow writer Dorothy Sayers, Burrage bemoans how War is War "promised to be a great success, but was only a moderate one". The book itself was received with reviews on both sides of the spectrum. Cyril Fall's War Books, a survey of post-war writing published in 1930, gives a clear indication as to why the critics were so mixed in reception of the book. He writes:

This book is extremely uneven in quality. The account of the attack at Paschendaele and of conditions at Cambrai after the great German counter-attack are very good indeed; in fact among the best of their kind. But the rest is disfigured by an unreasoned and unpleasant attack on superiors and all troops other than those of the front line, which is all the more astonishing because the author is inclined to harp upon his social position as compared with that of many of the officers with whom he came in contact. He does not use as much bad language as many writers on the War, but his methods of abuse will leave on some of his readers at least a worse impression than the most highly-spiced language.

Dorothy Sayers was the editor at Victor Gollanz for anthologies of ghost and horror stories which included stories by Burrage. She says, in one of her letters of Burrage's story The Waxwork, a piece beyond the nerves of the editors, "what you say about "The Waxwork" sounds very exciting, just the sort of thing I want. Our nerves are stronger than those of the editors of periodicals, and we will publish anything, so long as it does not bring us into conflict with the Home Secretary". Though their correspondence began as strictly business, Burrage's acquaintance with Atherton Fleming, Sayers's husband, allowed their interactions to become less formal and friendlier. Burrage wrote of Fleming "I hope to encounter him soon in one of the Fleet Street tea-shops". 'Tea-shop' being a popular euphemism for the pub, where both Burrage and Fleming could frequently be found, though their alcohol consumption came to damage both their health and their professions, with Burrage coming off the worse.

Happily for Burrage, as a result of being featured in one of Sayers's anthologies, The Waxwork became one of his best-known stories and it would grab the attention of the film companies several times down the years even becoming an episode in the TV series 'Alfred Hitchcock Presents'.

The developing friendship between Burrage and Sayers enabled him to reveal more details of his personal life, admitting to her his "neuritis at both ends (legs and eyes)", and hinting at his troubles with alcohol: "Fleet Street is not a good place for a man who delights in succumbing to temptation, and whose doctor says that even small doses of alcohol are poison to him". Sayers sympathises, replying that Fleming "agrees with you entirely about the temptations of Fleet Street; he has, however, succeeded, through sheer strength of character, in being able to drink soda-water in the face of all his fellow journalists".

In another of Burrage's letters, he apologises for a delay in sending proofs of a story, with the words:

I have had a pretty thin time lately through illness and anxiety. And for days on end haven't had the energy in me to write a letter, and when I had the energy to send a complete set of proofs to you I found I hadn't the postage money (This is when you take out your handkerchief and start sobbing). I owed my late agent over £1000, so I got practically nothing out of War is War. He stuck to it. Well, he is paid off now, and so are my arrears of income tax. All this took a toll of my very small earning capacity, and I have been sold up. This on top of something which promised to be a great success and was only a moderate one, was a bit too much for me. Still, in spite of sickness I am resilient and shall float again. "You can't keep a good man down," as the whale said about Jonah.

For a man who had so many stories in so many magazines, and was gaining pace in Sayers's anthologies as a talented writer of horror stories, his income will have been far higher than the then average wage, and yet as he says, he finds himself short of money.

Several questions are left unanswered about his personal life. It is unclear whether he was still supporting family, or whether he spent the majority of his money on alcohol, or whether he chose to conceal his true fortunes from those around him. Perhaps most incongruous is the apparent absence of a wife; though his death certificate indicates that he had one, listed as H.A. Burrage, he seems never to mention her to Sayers.

He was around forty-two when he wrote that apology letter to Sayers, though in tone and circumstance it seems to be from a man in a far later stage of his life.

Burrage continued writing until his death in 1956, and continued to be prolifically published. Indeed, the Evening News alone published some forty of his stories between 1950-56. His death is recorded at Edgware General Hospital on 18th December, and the causes of his death are recorded as congestive cardiac failure, arteriosclerosis and chronic bronchitis. He was sixty-seven years old, and his last address is listed as 105 Vaughan Road, Harrow.

Though his name is not often remembered in lists of prominent writers of his time, or even it's genres, his ghost stories are highly regarded by critics and fans alike, while his life story tells us much about the trials and stresses placed on authors during and after the war, and on soldiers returning from that war. His reluctant acceptance that the money was in the magazines while the esteem was in the poorly-paying hard covers, and his persistence as a writer, speak of a determined man, doomed to circumstance yet living as best he could.

In ending A.M Burrage wrote a few sentences which best sum up two things. Firstly his love for his son Simon (who sadly passed away in October 2013 and was a great and passionate advocate for his Father's works.) and secondly his succinct reasons for writing.

TO JULIAN SIMON FIELD BURRAGE
who at the moment of writing will
soon achieve the great age of four.
From somebody who loves him.

In War is War I admitted being a professional writer, or in other words one who depends for his bread and cheese and beer on writing, typing or dictating strings of sentences which his masters, the Public, are kind enough to buy and presumably to read.

The book brought me letters from a few old friends and a great many new ones. A large percentage of the new friends, who missed having seen that my identity was rather unkindly betrayed by the Press, wrote and asked (a) who I was and (b) what sort of stories did I write?

The answer to the second question will be found in the following pages. The answer to the first question is 'Nobody Much', worse luck.

Most of these stories were written with the intention of giving the reader a pleasant shudder, in the hope that he will take a lighted candle to bed with him—for candle-makers must be considered in these hard times. Some have already made their bow from the pages of the monthly magazines. The best have, quite naturally, been rejected.